Namaste AmeriKa

DEEPA MEHTA

iUniverse®

NAMASTE AMERIKA

iUniverse books may be ordered through booksellers or by contacting:

iUniverse
1663 Liberty Drive
Bloomington, IN 47403
www.iuniverse.com
1-800-Authors (1-800-288-4677)

ISBN: 978-1-4917-8334-4 (sc)
ISBN: 978-1-4917-8335-1 (e)

Library of Congress Control Number: 2015919153

Print information available on the last page.

iUniverse rev. date: 12/02/2015

This book is a work of fiction. Names, characters, places and incidents are products of the author's imagination or are used fictitiously. Any resemblance to actual events or locales or persons living or dead is entirely coincidental.

Special Thanks......

To Malou Wagner, my editor,
for all your encouragement,
your generosity with your time and energy,
and most of all your patience.

To My Mother

Very Special Thanks to my loving Mother
For her counsel, for the safe haven of her protection
And the relief from responsibility
which trusting in her
Judgment always gave me.

Table of Contents

Namaste AmeriKa

1. In the Plane

Snow is still falling. Sonya and Shahil are worrying about the trip. They have been preparing for the trip for the last two months. It was just last night they heard the news of the unexpected snowfall of about 15 inches.

They can't even call the limousine company as their office was closed due to heavy snow fall. Having brought all the baggage to the garage, they are eagerly awaiting the limousine. They did a final check up on the house to turn on the alarm.

Suri and Krish are chasing after each other and throwing snowballs to each other. They are in their happy mood to go on a long vacation. Suri, now 12 years-old is still acting like a child, and Krish is only eight. They keep chasing each other and running around the house.

"Mom, says Krish, "Suri took my game and hid it somewhere, I can't find it." Sonya turns around, "Come on kids, it's not the time for complaints. Pack up, and get ready."

Just about that time, Shahil points to the arrival of the limousine, and is relieved that they are finally able to make their trip. He was wondering about what would happen if the limousine didn't come? Who would be able to drop them to the airport in this kind of weather? "Sonya, Krish, Suri come on, get into the car." He manages to put all the baggage into the car.

The limousine is running slowly due to the heavy snow on the road. In fact, the driver had to make a couple more stops to pick up other passengers. Now, the limousine is running slowly but steadily. Krish and Suri fell asleep, since they woke up early in the morning.

All of a sudden, Shahil senses that something is wrong. The driver slams on the break, and the car turns around, sliding on the ice. The driver is very upset and says this happens for the first time in his life. He has been driving for twenty years now, and so far he hasn't had any accidents. Shahil replies calmly, "Don't worry, we understand the situation." After a few minutes, the driver starts the car again. Within an hour, they finally arrive at the JFK airport in New York. Shahil says to Sonya, "Thank the Lord, we are here." They take the luggage out of the limousine's trunk and put it on a cart.

They take place on a wooden bench in the waiting area. Krish goes to the vending machine to get soda and chips. After half an hour of waiting, Shahil hears the announcement: "Air India – 101 is ready, please get ready for the luggage check". They get ready with the passports and tickets.

The line is extremely long. After half an hour, it's the Mehras' turn; their passports and tickets get checked, and the luggage is put on the rolling track. Shahil silently observes that the security check is very tough these days. After the 911 attacks, wherever you go, the security check becomes tougher and more time consuming. After the security check, Sonya, Shahil, Suri and Krish board the Air India 101. Shahil checks his family seat numbers. They get their seats near the window. But there is one window in a row, and Krish and Suri both want a window seat. They both argue until Krish makes a deal with Suri, "Ok, I get the window seat for three hours, and then you can have it for three hours." They both agreed.

Krish is flying for the first time so he is very excited. He wants to see the big New York City from his window. It would be fun for him to see the New York City view from the sky. Since it is nighttime, New York City is lighted all around. Just then an announcement was heard: "The plane is ready to take off; please fasten the seatbelt". All passengers start to fasten the seatbelt. The airhostess passes by each row to check if everybody has fastened the belt.

The plane enters the runway and in a few minutes takes off. Krish, curiously, keeps looking out of the window just to see how it takes off. In a few minutes, plane is up in the air. New York City is full of lights, looking so beautiful. Krish and Suri are looking at the beautiful tall buildings and the roads and highways with high traffic. Cars are driving so fast that it looks like everybody is in a rush to get home.

Shortly, New York City disappears from the window view. Now that the children can see nothing but clouds, Krish says, "Mom, I can't see anything but clouds. It's no fun to sit at the window." Sonya said, "Krish, don't complain so much. You will fall asleep soon. You must be tired by now." Krish says nothing and starts to play his video game. The stewardess comes to their seats and serves some snacks and juice. After the snack service is finished, the lights are turned off. Shahil reads a magazine in dim light. Suri is already in sleep, and Krish is falling asleep too; Sonya takes the videogame from his hand and slowly puts the air pillow around his neck.

Sonya is quiet and watches Krish's cute face while asleep. He has fair skinned face with black curly hair. He is eight years but still so cute, so innocent looking young child that she can't stop staring at him; he is sweet heart to her. Shahil is tired from the long day waiting and falls asleep quickly. Sonya holds his hand and closes her eyes trying to sleep. She fall asleep in few minutes.

Half an hour passes and Sonya is heard screaming in her dreams: "Shahil, Shahil, are you there? Are you there? I saw the police…They will take you away." Sonya is crying. Her cheeks are red; her eyes are full of tears. She looks around as if someone is about to take Shahil away from her.

Shahil wakes up from his sleep unsure of what has happened, but he heard the scream. He soothes her, "Sonya, I am right here with you and nobody is going to take me away from you." He puts his hand around Sonya's neck, and puts her head over his shoulder. Quickly, two stewardesses come to check on her and ask, "Are you ok, Sir"? Is she ok, Sir? Are you comfortable? The stewardess brings two spring water bottles and tells them to take it easy. Shahil thanks them, and then stares at Sonya's face, looking a little worried. What would it be like, without his dear Sonya?

Sonya tries to feign sleep. In fact, she acts as she snores a little to show that she is truly falling asleep, so Shahil can sleep without worrying about her. After a few minutes, Shahil is indeed asleep, while Sonya was awake. Sonya goes into deep thoughts about her past. The more she thinks about it, the more tears run down her cheeks. Am I really going back to my home land with my husband or is that a dream? What if something happens while she is on her way home? She isn't able to trust herself, despite the fact that she is on the plane with Shahil and her two kids to see her homeland for the first time in 15 years of their marriage. Her family members and the in-laws haven't seen Krish yet, and Suri was so little when they saw her. Will her dream come true this time around? She is nearly shaken and more tears are running down her face.

2. Trip canceled

It was November 1992. Sonya, Shahil and the children were all prepared to go to Shahil's only nephew's wedding back in their homeland. Sonya was well prepared with her beautiful dresses to wear in the wedding parade, the wedding, the reception, and in so many other rituals that are part of the wedding ceremony. She was so excited to go to the wedding with Shahil, since it was the first wedding occasion after her marriage in her in-law's family. She bought beautiful jewelry for the occasion, and chose what kind of hairstyles she would make and what kind of make up she would wear in each ceremony.

They bought many gifts for each family member and for each friend. Shahil bought a few suits for his nephew's wedding as well as different types of perfumes and other gifts for the special groom to be. It was his pleasure to make everything right at this occasion.

During this preparation time, they would get phone calls from families to check that everything was ready, especially with regards to Krish, who was only 3 months old. All the family members had seen newborn Krish's picture. They just couldn't wait to see him personally. They were wondering, if Krish's pictures are so beautiful, what would be Krish like. Shahil was the youngest child of his seven brothers and sisters, and he was dearest to all of his family members. And Krish, the interest of the principal? They just couldn't wait to see and hold their Shahil's little prince, Krish. Shahil's mom advised him to make sure Krish doesn't catch a cold or a fever while traveling. They advised him to get enough baby food that Krish likes. They wanted to make sure that Krish should not be uncomfortable in the new atmosphere at home.

When Sonya got phone calls from family members about Krish, she felt very happy to hear them talk about Krish. She remembered the time when she was in the hospital with Krish. When Krish was born, Sonya wasn't even well enough to see him properly. She just looked at him and thought, "Oh, my God, he is so cute." He had born with long, curly black hair. His eyes were long, big and with long eyelashes. He looked so cute when he was sleeping. Due to a misunderstanding, she unfortunately told the nurse to bring him only for feeding for a day or two, so she could rest. But that day or two was so long for her that she thought she made a mistake to sign the papers to let them keep the child and bring him only for feeding time. When the nurse would bring Krish to her, they would say: "Here is your handsome boy. He is so cute. Have fun!" After an hour, the nurse would come to take Krish back. Sonya would ask her if she could keep him longer, but the nurse would say, "No ma'm, sorry, you have signed the papers and we have to follow the procedure." After the nurse left, she would wait eagerly for the little cute baby to come back. Every 15 minutes, Sonya would walk from her room to the lobby, and check whether is time for him to come back and felt sorry that it wasn't a time for him to come back. She could hardly wait for the two days to pass in order to hold him tight. She should have rested during that time, but she just couldn't.

After two days, she was dismissed from the hospital, and he was all hers for all day and night to play with. She would try to make him laugh and stare at him while he was asleep. Time just passed by so quickly and now she was all ready to go on a long trip.

Suri, then four years old, was excited to see his cousin, who was getting married soon. She was going to be the chief guest for all her family members. Everybody loved her so dearly, so she was going to get the most attention from all her uncles and aunts and especially from her grandmother. She was well prepared with her little dresses and other little things. Suri also got some little gifts and candies for her little friends back home. Suri would talk to everybody on the phone in her sweet and cute language, which made Sonya a proud mother. Sonya prepared her to perform a dance at the wedding parade on Ballet song. Sonya made her practice almost everyday evening after dinner.

Shahil and Sonya went to sleep late at night after all the bags were packed. Sonya checked on Krish in his baby crib, covered him properly with his beautiful, sky blue teddy bear designed baby comforter, and kissed his head and cheek. She checked on Suri, who was sleeping with her dear teddy bear as well.

Sonya kissed her head too. After all the checks, she went to bed. Shahil and Sonya were both tired by now. It was almost 2.00 a.m., Shahil said, "Sonya, there are only three days left to go home. You will be free from work and house chores, and will be visiting friends and families and enjoying wedding occasion. It's something you've been waiting for." Sonya responds, "I can't wait for that happy time to arrive."

They chatted a little while longer. Shahil hugged her, and kissed her cheek and lips. Shortly afterwards, both were asleep, waiting for the long vacation trip home.

The next morning, Shahil went to work. Today was the last day of work before the vacation, so he took some cake, snacks, and soda for his co-workers. His partner, Mr. CJ, was kidding around with him. "Oh, yeah he doesn't have to work today." He told Shahil, "Just enjoy and have fun today. Next month I will see you. I will be on vacation, and you will be working," and he laughed. All day he passed in relaxed meetings with other co-workers, chatting, and joking around. When he went home he had some final check on his trip, so he got busy. They had to leave early the next day.

They had dinner around 6.45 pm. After finishing all her chores in the kitchen, Sonya called Suri. "Would you please do your last practice on your dance?

Hesitatingly, Suri said, "Mom, can I skip it today? I can do my dance. I won't make any mistakes, Mom. Please.........mom........"

Sonya: "Honey, just one more practice and you will be done for this wedding." Suri agreed, so Sonya put an audiotape in the stereo system and started the music to play on song.

The song began, and Suri started to dance. As she was working on her dance, Sonya corrected her pose and movements. "Ok...stop...not this way...this is better, showing her ballet style hand and feet posture. Yeah... right...this is perfect. Good job, Suri." Suri did it again and again. She was almost done.

There was a knock at the door. Sonya heard it, but couldn't pay attention while she was working on the dance. Knock ...knock...another knocking voice she heard. She stopped the music and went to open the door. It was around 8.00 pm. She wondered who it could be at this time of the night. She wasn't expecting anyone but she opened..... the..... door......!

The police? … She screamed … She saw the police in front of the door, and she was scared. Now, why are they here? Her heartbeat was racing; she was sweating on this cold November night. She hid her feelings and scared facial expression. She put a fake little smile on, and asked them politely, "Yes sir, how can I help you? Her leaps were shaking and her eyes were rolling ups and down at the police officer.

"Is Mr. Shahil Mehra there?"

"Yes, Sir, he is in the house…come on in please," said Sonya.

She wondered why they wanted to talk to him, but she called him anyway.

Shahil walked in, "Yes, Sir?"

"Mr. Mehra, you are under arrest," said the two police detectives.

"What?" Shahil almost screamed.

"Why you are arresting me? What you have against me?" Shahil said. Police: "We have an arrest warrant for you."

"Arrest warrant? For what?" Shahil was utterly surprised.

"You are leaving the country, and you may not come back," said the detectives.

"But, Sir," Shahil said, "I have given my date to your department a long time before. I haven't hidden anything and I am not lying to anyone." He was very upset and sweating. He tried to talk to them, "Look my bags are ready, my passport, my tickets…my wife and children are going too. My baby boy is just three months old, sir, what are you doing?" His hands were trembling, and his eyes were watery.

The two detectives were smiling at each other as if they were giving each other a sign. They started to handcuff Shahil, while he kept saying, "Sir, your department has returned the passport. Why are you here last minute?"

"Just shut up, just shut up, said the two detectives and they started to push him towards the door. They were pushing him so hard that Shahil tripped at the entrance. He hurt his knee and started to bleed, but he controlled himself and said, "Just don't push me. I am coming with you."

Sonya almost stopped breathing, and stood there like a statue listening to their conversation. Then she started to cry. "Help, someone help." But who would listen to her? It was nighttime. The street was quiet, and mostly dark with some streetlights. Everybody must be at home watching TV or getting ready for bed.

She stopped Shahil, "Oh please, don't leave me. Don't leave the children." She cried hard and bent down on her knees. Little Suri was there, not knowing what was going on. She started to cry too.

Shahil was six feet tall and a handsome young man. He never cried in his life, but looking at Sonya's situation he started to cry. While he was going with the police, he told Sonya, "Don't worry. Hire a lawyer right away." He left with the detectives in their car. Crying hard, Sonya watched the car leave, her hands up in the air, screaming "Shahil...Shahil...Shahil."

Finally, she had to get up and went inside the house. She didn't know what to do at this time. She was thinking of all the preparations they had made for the last month or so, of the wedding, of the family back home. What would she say to them when they knew that Shahil's family would not arrive as they had scheduled? At this time, they would all be prepared to go to the airport to receive Shahil's family. They were eager to see Shahil's little baby boy. How would she explain to them that they were not coming? She couldn't even contact a lawyer until the next morning. She sighed deeply. Tomorrow, they are supposed to leave, but instead she would be seeing a lawyer. What bad luck!

3. Dr. Ashish's trip

Sonya's brother-in-law, who was a doctor in California, was also leaving for the trip to attend the wedding in India. Sonya thought she should talk to them about Shahil's arrest.

Quickly, she dialed the number with trembling hands. How would she talk to her brother-in-law, Dr. Ashish Mehra? How he would feel? Maybe he would cancel the trip from his side. Who would help her? There is nobody in this country other than the brother-in-law from the family. Tears were rolling down her face, while she was thinking about what to tell her only brother-in-law and only family member.

"Hello," says a familiar voice on the other end.

"Oh, thank God he is there," Sonya thought. For few moments, she couldn't talk. Dr. Ashish Mehra said hello a couple times. Finally, she spoke to him, "Hello brother, it's me, Sonya."

"Hi Sonya, how are you? What's up? Is everything ready?" "No, brother," she broke off and started to cry before she could mention anything to him.

"Why are you crying? What happened? Why don't you say something?" Still crying, Sonya tried to stop in order to speak. Finally, she said, "Shahil has been arrested." "What?" said Dr. Mehra. "What was the reason? Why on the last day of the trip? Did you talk to them?"

Sonya explained the whole situation and said, "Brother, can you please cancel your trip? A brief silence followed on the other end. "Let me think about it first. In the meantime, why don't you hire a lawyer?"

In the background, she heard the voice of her sister-in- law Piyasi, saying to him that no matter what happens, she wants to go. She will not cancel the trip.

"Brother, I don't know how to hire a lawyer. I have never been in this kind of situation in my life, and I am pretty new to this country. Where would I go? And how would I hire a lawyer?"

"Look Sonya, just check the yellow pages, pick one and call. Make an appointment and talk to the lawyer."

Sonya started to cry hard, begging him not to leave her alone. What I will tell our big brother back home?

Dr. Mehra said, "Sonya, don't worry, I will talk to them. Here, I'll put Piyasi on the phone. Talk to her."

Piyasi, his wife, took the phone and started to show her emotions. She was crying too. "Sonya, I am very sorry that you won't be able to come. Please take it easy. Everything will be fine. We will come back in 15 days, and we will visit you." Sonya was still crying, and couldn't say anything to her. Piyasi continued, "We didn't mean to hurt you. My brother and I tried our best for Shahil. And Sonya, please don't call our brother-in-law back home. I will tell them that Shahil had an accident, so he couldn't come." Sonya just said ok and hung up.

In fact, Sonya knew that her devious sister-in-law had a plan. She just wanted to look good in front of all the in- laws. She clearly wanted to lie about what was going on for the last several months. Shahil was everyone's favorite and the family members wouldn't enjoy wedding without him. There would be thousands of questions from everybody as to Shahil's whereabouts, and she had to make up a story.

Sonya was circling in her bedroom, thinking about what to do at this critical time. It was time to feed little Krish, but she didn't even think about him until he cried. She gave him a milk bottle, and then she turned on the musical toy attached to his crib, which put him to sleep.

All of a sudden, she came to the conclusion that no matter what Piyasi said to her, she must let her elder brother-in-law know about the situation and about their canceled trip. As she was about to dial his number, she despaired at the thought of telling her own family and relatives, especially her grandfather, who was eagerly waiting to see her for the last five years. She decided not to tell them at all. Her brother-in-law would tell them whatever he decided to tell them.

She dialed the number again, and her nephew, the groom-to-be, picked up the phone. There was so much noise coming from around the house due to lots of invited guest. To her, it sounded like everybody was laughing and joking with each other, having fun. Some music was going on too. Her nephew said, "Hi Aunty, we are eagerly waiting for you. Please, don't call us. We just want to see you now." Are you all ready now to come in my wedding? Sonya didn't respond to the comment, but asked to speak to her brother-in-law. He found it odd that Aunt Sonya didn't want to talk to him; he handed the phone over to his father. Sonya's brother-in-law Roshan took the phone, and Sonya, with a broken heart, told him about the situation. She asked him not to mention anything to anyone at this occasion.

He couldn't believe what he heard. He broke down, his heart was crying, but he couldn't cry since so many guests were around the house. He thought about the wedding of his only son, and how his dearest Shahil wouldn't attend the special wedding. It was very hard for him to believe what happened to Shahil, his dear brother's situation. When he heard that his other brother, Dr. Ashish, is coming, he became angry but he couldn't do anything. He just had to watch the time approaching. Many thoughts raced through his mind. How would he tell his wife, and especially his mother, who was very eager to see Shahil and his little Krish and Suri. He had to manage no matter what. Finally, he decided to talk to his immediate family members. He told his wife as well as his only son that Shahil had an accident and he wouldn't be able to attend the wedding.

Everybody was upset and started to worry about his health. Will he be alright? What if he is badly injured? Who will take care of him? His mother started to cry and went to another room. She just couldn't think of the family's big wedding occasion without Shahil, her youngest and dearest child of all. In a few hours, the rumor had gone around town that Shahil had an accident and wouldn't be able to come. Everybody started to talk about Shahil. It was a small town and most people knew Shahil's well-known family, their wedding and the most gorgeous wedding settings in the town. Some people even said that accidents are very common in America, since there are a lot of vehicles on the road. They felt sorry to hear about Shahil's accident. Some friends and relatives came to console Shahil's big brother.

As the situation developed at Sonya's in-laws', the news went at her family's house. Sonya didn't even call them, but the rumor went around and her family members heard the news. They became upset, thinking they meant nothing to Sonya that she didn't tell them anything. Shouldn't she tell them first as they are her brothers and sisters? They came to the conclusion that after the marriage, she changed a lot. They are nothing to her and her in-laws are everything to her. Even though everyone was upset with her, they felt pity for her situation as well. They worried how she would handle everything alone with two little kids. One after another, they started to call her.

It was late at night. Sonya was trying to sleep but couldn't. It was for the first time she was alone and it was hard for her to be alone in her king size bed. Her thoughts focused on the detectives again. How would they treat Shahil? What would be tonight like for him? The first thing she had to take care of tomorrow was to find a lawyer. If she finds one, how will the lawyer respond to her? Would he/she be cooperative? Would he/she believe her part of the story? What if her case wouldn't be accepted? How many lawyers will she have to contact? What would be the cost to accept this kind of case? Questions kept creeping up. Her body was shaking with cold in her bed even though there was enough heat in the house.

She never had to deal with a lawyer or the police in her entire life. She belonged to one of the best caste systems of India. She never heard of this situation happening to anyone she knew of. Even if people heard about such a scandal, they would put a finger on their mouth, and say "Sh…sh….sh…h…h…." They would not talk in public about this kind of case. It was just Shameful to think about little stealing. What they would think about the arrest? Now that she had to deal with a lawyer, it would be very hard to explain everything. Would she be able to speak up? What would happen next and then next and then next? Sonya couldn't think more. She turned around, her face on the pillow, and shut her eyes while she was crying alone in bed. Sonya spent the night without sleeping twisting and turning.

4. The first appointment

It was a cold November morning. She got up early, took a bath and got ready. She didn't even feel to take her regular coffee and breakfast. She made a list of lawyers and phone numbers taken from the yellow pages, and started to call lawyers' offices one after another. Most lawyers' offices couldn't give her an appointment right away. Some of them were very busy or didn't seem to be interested. Her last resort was to call her work's union office. They provided a phone number of a lawyer who was a registered with the union. She got an appointment with him on the same day. She got ready to go to the lawyer's office, located in Center City Philadelphia. She never drove on the expressway, so she decided to take the train.

She was very tired because she couldn't sleep all night. While she was traveling, she felt sleepy, but how could she possibly sleep? She was preparing her address to the lawyer. How would the lawyer react towards her? Would he be nice enough to listen to what she had to say? Would he give her enough time to explain the situation? What about the lawyer's fee? It worried her the most. No matter what the fees would be, she had to hire the lawyer. In 45 minutes, she was in Center City looking for the building she wrote down on a slip of paper. All her life she lived in beautiful suburb of Philadelphia. It's the naturally Beautiful, quiet and safest location for her family. It was very hard for her to find streets and blocks of Center City high rise buildings. Finally, she found the building and went in the elevator to go up the 21st floor of a high-rise building. Her heart started to beating hard as she was thinking to see lawyer for the first time in her life. As she reached the 21st floor, elevator door opened and she came out to Lobby. She found the lawyer's office.

She directly went to the receptionist and told her about her appointment with the lawyer. "Please be seated. It will take a few minutes. Mr. Arthur is still with another client." said the receptionist. Sonya sat down on the sofa, but she couldn't sit comfortably for even a minute. She was so impatient and worried about the whole situation. She tried to pass time by watching the cityscape from the huge big window of the high-rise building. The beautiful oil paints, hanging over the wall of the receptionist area attracted her for a moment and she got lost in it. Shortly afterwards, the receptionist called her name and told her to go to the private conference room. She impatiently got up and went in.

"Hello, Mrs. Sonya Mehra," said Mr. Arthur.

He stood up and shook hands with Sonya.

"I am Mr. Phillip Arthur. What can I do for you?"

"I want to hire a lawyer."

"What for? Divorce? Or any thing else?" Mr. Arthur looked straight into her eyes.

"No, it's not divorce; it's a very serious matter. It's about my husband. He has been arrested," she said slowly.

"Why has he been arrested?" What has he done?

Sonya took a long deep breath and closed her eyes for a moment.

"He has done nothing... It's just...it's just..." She couldn't talk and started to cry. Philip Arthur was quiet for a moment, let her cry, and told her to calm down. After a few minutes, he continued with his inquiry. "If he has done nothing, why are you here? Why has he been arrested?"

Still crying, she responds, "He has been arrested for...for...hum...hum."

She couldn't finish her sentence.

"Could you please say something, Ms. Mehra? We lawyers don't have much time to waste. If you are unable to explain your situation within the time limit, I will have to charge you extra for my consultation time.

Sonya finally said in broken words, "for m..u..r.. for m..u..r..d..e..r."

"What?" Mr. Phillip Arthur nearly stood up in disbelief.

He didn't expect a young lady, beautiful and innocent like a dove, come to him for a criminal case. He had seen so many clients in his life during his practice as a lawyer, but this looked rather unusual to him. A criminal outlook would tell him, Yes, I am here for your help. But looking at Sonya, she looked like she came from a good family background. He simply couldn't fathom why she was here or what her husband could possibly have done?

"Can you tell me in detail when and why it happened? And what's against him that he has been arrested?" Mr. Phillip Arthur said. Slowly, Sonya started to explain the situation in detail.

After listening to Sonya, Mr. Arthur told her, "Ms. Mehra, I will charge you $10,000 in advance for the first hearing, and then if you want to continue with my service, I will charge you an extra $20,000 to finish the case." Sonya closed her eyes to think for a moment, but she knew she had no choice. She had to hire the lawyer in order for Shahil to get better service.

At this point, she didn't even know about the free lawyers that the court provides. Even if she would hire a free lawyer, would they care as much as private lawyers? In fact, she didn't know anything about court services and other lawyers in practice in town. The police and the court are a rare thing to think about in her life. She was very happy with Shahil and her two children, Suri and Krish. She never heard of anyone in her community in which she grew up of being engaged in this kind of activity. Why had she such bad luck to be forced to see a lawyer, and deal with the court and the police? She hated the situation she was in.

"Ms. Mehra, what are you thinking?"

"Oh…I am sorry…" She woke up from her thoughts. Y..e..s…yes… I am fine with your fees."

She thought she had no choice, especially since she didn't know anyone else. Who would she go to? Mr. Arthur told her to see her husband as soon as possible; he would make an appointment in the correctional facility, where the detectives held him. She thanked him and left the office to go home. She wanted to talk to Shahil about hiring the lawyer and his appointment with the lawyer the next day. But she couldn't talk, as she didn't know exactly where he was or how to contact him by phone. Ultimately, she expected the lawyer to take care of the rest.

5. Sonya in puzzle

Sonya was tired from last night and she wanted to take a nap. As she came home from the lawyer's office, she changed her dress, and went to her bedroom. Before she goes to bed, She told her mother not to bother her for a couple hours.

Since yesterday night, she even didn't care to check on little Krish, who was four months old now. As Krish saw his mom, he raised his hand to indicate that he wanted to be picked up. He was smiling at her and kicking his feet in joy to see her. What did he know about her pain? Sonya saw his sweet and cute smile and for a moment, she forgot her painful situation. She picked him up and hugged him dearly. She mumbled to herself, "Oh, sweetheart, I am so sorry, I don't have time for you." She wasn't in the mood to play with Krish, so after few minutes she gave him to her mother.

Her mother came to the USA on a visiting visa to help Sonya with her delivery time. She was supposed to go back home two months after Krish's birth. She wanted to see her two grand children and also give her daughter enough rest after the pregnancy. Since Sonya and Shahil were going to attend their nephew's wedding ceremony, they decided to take her with them. That way they could take care of her health during the long travel. All of a sudden, a crisis emerged in Sonya's life and she had to postpone her trip back home; she had no choice. Looking at Sonya's situation, she was the only family member to worry about her. Shahil was not here and Sonya would have to go to work. Who would take care of the children? How she would manage by herself to drop off and pick up the children from daycare on time? Since Shahil wouldn't have a job, what about the extra burden on Sonya? Would Sonya be able to look after the children properly in this kind of stress and tension? In fact, she had to take care of Sonya more than the children as Sonya had succumbed to a period of mental depression. She decided to stay with her daughter until Shahil would come back. She was a widow and single, so she had nothing much to worry about other than to see her grownup children and other family members occasionally.

Sonya was lying in bed trying to sleep for a couple hours. She recalled that today was the day to go back to her homeland. Instead of lying in bed, she would have been on the plane with her family flying towards home. By tonight, she would have seen all her brothers and sisters and in-laws, who were coming to receive them at the Bombay airport. Her eyes welling with tears, she thought about how hard they tried to be honest throughout the process; yet, nothing worked. It seemed like this world was for dishonest people and not for honest people. The more you tried to be nice, the more you got into trouble. There wasn't anyone to convince. What else could Shahil do? In a few minutes, she fell asleep, tired, worried, and in a stressful situation, which was going to stay with her God knows how many years.

6. Mr. Arthur

It was another cold November morning. The leaves on the trees were red and yellow, ready to say goodbye to summer. Mr. Arthur was looking out to his yard through the window of his family room. He was amazed to see the beauty of the fall season. While he was standing there, he thought about interviewing Mr. Mehra first thing in the morning. He got ready for his new client, laying out what he would ask him. He prepared his mind for the questions and answers, so he could set an appointment for the first hearing in the court. Maybe Mr. Mehra could be released on bail, or maybe not? It all depends on the facts he would gather in today's interview. He put on his long coat and went outside to start his Mercedes.

After a half hour drive, he came to the correctional facility to see Shahil Mehra. He contacted one of the correctional officers and told him about his appointment with Shahil Mehra. The officer told him to wait in the sitting area until he was called. After fifteen minutes, Mr. Arthur was allowed to see Shahil in a private room, where they could talk to each other face to face.

One of the correctional officers brought Shahil to the private meeting room. Shahil was sitting in the conference chair, waiting for his lawyer. Shahil was glad to meet the lawyer who was going to take care of his case. While he was waiting for him, he worried about explaining the situation to him. Many thoughts began racing through his mind. Would the lawyer believe him? He hadn't had any contact with Sonya since the night he was arrested. Did Sonya have a chance to tell him everything, or do I have to explain him everything? Sonya has never been in this kind of situation before. She is just a 30-year-old woman, a mother of two, but still a young woman. How would she be able to narrate everything in a short meeting? Anyway, I will have to tell him everything from beginning to end, he thought.

Phillip Arthur entered to the meeting room. There wasn't anyone else besides Shahil, so it didn't take him much time to recognize Shahil.

"Hello, Mr. Mehra, I am Phillip Arthur." He shook his hand.

"I am Shahil," said Shahil and he shook his hand. He felt happy to see him, as he detected in Philip Arthur a strong and determined person taking care of his case. Mr. Phillip evaluated Shahil from head to toe at one glance. Shahil was young, handsome, and 6 ft. tall. The way he was looking at him, it looked like the lawyer was trying to figure something out. After a brief introduction, both took seats opposite each other. Mr. Arthur began the questioning and took notes at the same time.

"Mr. Mehra, you are charged for murder. Is that correct?"

"Yes, Sir," said Shahil.

"Tell me about how you got involved in this case." He started to listen carefully as Shahil began to tell his part of the story.

7. Shahil tells story

In March of 1992, Jay, my brother-in-law, got killed somewhere near his work in North Philadelphia. Jay was my brother Dr. Ashish Mehra's brother-in-law (Piyasi's brother), and he had been living in Philadelphia since 1989. One day he left the house early in the morning to work overtime. That night he didn't come back home. His two brothers were also living with him in the same apartment. They called me, and told me that Jay had not come home yet. I thought he might have gone to a friend's house. So I told them to call some of his friend; he might have stopped there for short meeting. His brothers called his friend's house; their response was Jay didn't come to their house. His brother called one of his own friends, who also worked with Jay at the same place. His friend told him that Jay never came to work at all.

His brothers called me again and filled me in on the information. It was strange to hear that he left early for work in the morning and never arrived at work. Something must be wrong. I told them I would be there soon; I'd still make a couple phone calls myself. Finally, I called my brother in California and told him about Jay's disappearance. My brother advised me to report it to the police. I called the police; they came after an hour and took the report. They told us that he is an adult, and that he may just have left the house. There was nothing to be done at that time. Meanwhile, my brother and I kept in touch as to what to do. He also called the police from his house.

After many inquiries, we got a response from the police department around at 11 p.m. They told us that they found a person whose description is matching the one we gave them. They asked his brothers to identify the person. As I was the only relative here with them, so I accompanied them. They were still pretty young; and they wouldn't know what to do.

The three of us went to the homicide division and met with the police officer. They showed us a body over a TV screen and we identified it as Jay's. We all started to cry; he was like my younger brother. We informed Ashish Mehra about Jay's death, and he decided to come to Philadelphia immediately. That night, I stayed with the two brothers until Ashish and Piyasi arrived.

The next morning, the police detectives came and asked more questions for the report. A lot of other relatives heard the news and started to come to see us. The detectives told us there are two witnesses in this case and they are working with them. According to them, they saw a sky blue old Japanese car with a Hispanic looking person dropping something near the railway tracks. Jay had some gold jewelry, a Seiko watch and cash on him. He was robbed to death. They treated the case as a robbery.

After the detectives left, everybody in the room discussed what they heard. My brother pointed out that I have a blue car too: "Don't say anything or you will get in trouble. We have nothing to do with it and we don't want to get in trouble. Just stay away from trouble." I had utmost respect for my brother, and I was always obedient to him. I lived with him for three years and I always felt grateful for that too. To show my respect, I nodded in agreement. My brother and I made the funeral arrangement. After the cremation, Jay's ashes had to be thrown into the Holy Ganges. Hence, someone had to go back to India to fulfill the holy rituals. Piyasi cried so hard, as she has a sick daughter, and thus won't be able to accompany her husband for the holy rituals. I pitied her situation, but I had just bought a business. I didn't have any money for an air ticket. Jay's two brothers were very upset; it was almost impossible to send one of them back home. One brother had to stay here since the police inquiry was going on. Piyasi heard about my financial situation and quickly suggested that they'd pay for the ticket. In the end, I flew to India to take care of the holy rituals, and returned to my family after 15 days.

Arthur was still listening patiently, as he wanted to understand why Shahil was arrested. Shahil sipped some water and continued narrating the event.

After returning home, I turned to my business as usual. One day, I was at the store, getting ready to go to bank for a deposit. I went to my car in the parking lot right outside the store. I tried to start the car, but it stalled. I asked my partner to give my car battery a jump. My partner tried to give my car battery a jump.

As it didn't work either, I called the AAA service for emergency help. They failed to start the car as well, so they towed it to the nearest gas station for repair.

I told the mechanic to give me a call for a repair estimate. He pointed out that they are pretty busy right now; he'd call as soon as they had time. I remember mentioning to him that my car is too old to put too much money in it. The next day, the mechanic called me and gave me an estimate of $700. Since my car's book value was only $300, I hesitated to make a decision. Ever since I arrived in the USA, I took advice from Ashish whenever I had to do something new. So I called my brother, and we discussed the car's repair costs. He told me, "Shahil, it's not worth it to put a single penny into that car. You have waited long enough to get a new car and it's a time for you to buy a new one."

I agreed. For the first few years, I saved money to buy a house. Now that I own a house and have been settled for a couple years, I should buy a new car. Also, I thought Sonya was pregnant, and thus we would need more room to put a baby seat in the car and for the baby's safe keeping, only to buy a new car would be better. After further deliberations, I told my wife that we are getting a new car. She was excited to hear the news. We both went to look at new cars at different auto dealers.

I called my mechanic and let him know that I didn't want my old car repaired. He asked me, "What you want to do with this car?" I asked him if I could get some money back for the car. The answer was no as the car was not worth to keep. "You will have to pay us to get rid of this car or just take it back home." I thought, if I would choose to take car home, I would have to pay for it. In the end, I told the mechanic to keep the car and take the parts that are still usable.

Arthur was quite amused. He thought to himself Shahil was not anywhere near the point he should be with his explanation. Clearing his throat, he asked, "What is the point for your arrest Mr. Shahil?"

Shahil took a deep breath and waited for a few minutes. With eyes tearing up he says, "The story starts now, Mr. Arthur. Just listen."

My wife and I rented a car for a couple days until we bought the new car. We went to so many different dealers to get the best price. My wife had a dream to get a Toyota Camry, so we both decided to buy that car. I returned to my business as usual. My four-year-old daughter, Sonya and I were happy with the choice of car. I talked to Ashish about the new car; he was fine with it.

After a couple days, Jay's youngest brother, Aryan, who was handling the case called to say hi. We talked for a while and I mentioned to him that we bought a new car. He didn't respond at all and hung up.

On the next day, he reported my name as a suspect, because I had a blue car. I didn't know anything about his report to police. That same evening, two detectives came to my store and ordered me to accompany them. I asked them why and where. They started to push me. "Just go with us. As to the why and where, you will soon know, Mr. Shahil." I wasn't sure what was going on. I just sat in their car.

Half an hour later, they took me to their office and put me in a closed room. Two detectives started to question me about Jay's killing. I told them I had nothing to do with it. Then they started to hit me. I kept telling them that I don't know anything. One detective hit me with his fist on my eyes. They took on dark circle. They kept hitting me to make me confess. After nearly four hours, they still didn't let me go. I asked them for some water. They didn't give me any. They asked the questions again and again. I was tired and thirsty, but they kept hitting me. At one point, they kicked the chair and I thrown out off the chair. It's been six hours and I wanted to go to restroom. They didn't let me go. Even when I wet my pants, they didn't let me go to the restroom. In another room, they kept my business partner to make reveal something about the car. They forced him to say something. He said that the car failed to start and they had to call the AAA emergency service for a tow truck. For six to eight hours, they kept hitting and torturing me to receive a confession. I didn't know anything, so what would I tell them?

Meanwhile, my wife called the store. As nobody picked up the phone, she started to worry. One hour after they took me, Sonya was bought to the same place where I was held. She was six month pregnant at that time. She was asked many questions in a rough manner. They started to interrogate her, yet her answer was the same. She told them that the three brothers were like my little brothers, and we had nothing to do with this. My wife couldn't sit any longer; she had her stomach ached. Nonetheless, they didn't stop the interrogation. To scare my wife, they told her that they found blood in my car. "Now you must confess that he did it." My wife said, "My husband couldn't even kill a rat, so there is nothing that I have to agree with you." After five hours, they let her go. Sonya couldn't stand properly due to the increased pain of sitting on a hard chair for so long. She was waiting for me in the hallway.

She started to worry about me, wondering why I was held responsible for something like this. She didn't even know that Aryan reported my name, because we bought a new car. We never had a problem with the three brothers; in fact, we always had a good relationship with them. Otherwise, why would they call us first on the day of Jay's disappearance?

When I came out of the room, Sonya saw me walking straight, with my head up and no trace of fear. She felt so good. She has known me for so many years and I couldn't hide anything from her – whether it was a small lie or the truth. She saw dark circles around my eyes and she started to cry. She said, "Shahil your mother and father never slapped your face. What am I seeing on your face?" She felt so sorry about what had happened to me. We were both terribly ashamed. That night we arrived home very late.

The following day I asked my brother to come to Philadelphia in order to go to the police station with me. My brother agreed to help me and flew to Philadelphia on the earliest plane. I told him that I wanted to take a lie detector test. Ashish thought it was only necessary if the case progresses any further. "You should worry then; right now they are just investigating you." In a confidential discussion, Ashish declared, "I don't believe that you have killed Jay, but in case you have, I advise you to run away to India. I don't want to see you in jail. You are my brother and I love you so much." Slightly shocked, I told him that I never committed a crime. "I don't know who did it and I was still pushing for the lie detector test. I also told him to give them my passport in case they thought I'd run away.

The next morning, we went to the police department and I asked them to take a lie detector test. They agreed to it and I was sent to the special division. The lady, who was reporting my name and other information, told me, "Sir, if you caught lying in this test, you will be in big trouble." I calmly responded, "I didn't do anything wrong, so I have nothing to worry about." She repeated a few more times, "Mr. Shahil, think again! You still have time to say no". Every time she asked me, I stuck with my decision to take the test.

Finally, I entered a special room and got hooked to the lie detector machine. I was asked several questions about Jay's killing. I gave each answer truthfully and told them what I knew. After one hour of questioning, they freed me and I had to wait outside for the lie-detector report. A lady came to me and said, "Congratulations, you have passed the test." Afterwards, my brother advised the two detectives not to hit or even to touch me again during their investigations. We went home and my brother flew back to California.

Now, I started my business as usual. They started to come to my home over and over again to check. Every time I was asked if I wanted to hire a lawyer, and I told them that I didn't need a lawyer because I was innocent.

I supported them in everything they wanted to check. During this time, I came to know that they detained my car from the gas station. They conducted a thorough search, and they even had a police dog go through my car. A few days later the report came out as: "No blood. No weapon found. No fiber match." The report clearly showed that my car was not involved in the murder. They found the tire print at the murder scene on the day of murder. The tests showed that the prints didn't match my car tire either.

Those two detectives and a couple others were coming to my house in different group. They questioned the worker at the gas station and forced him to testify against me. But the worker told them the truth: he had cheated me by raising the repair costs, so I would give up or sell my car to him at no cost. I really believed him and sold my car for no money. If I had known that the repair cost was only $250, I would have kept the car. But unfortunately, they lied and I got in trouble.

When all the investigations were over and they found nothing against me, two detectives came to my house and told me that it is all over and you are free. I asked them if I can have my passport back. They told me to come to the office and get the passport. On the next day I went to their office and asked for the passport. The two mean – spirited detectives were there and said, "Oh Mr. Mehra, congratulations! When are you going home?" I told them the correct date and month and went home.

Life went back to normal again; I continued to work at my store as usual. After a month or so, they called me into the office for a couple hours and asked the same questions over again. They went to my wife's office, and they took her with them. As she was pregnant, she wasn't able to sit for a long time. They started to interrogate her, and talked about cultures and so many other things. Sonya answered them as best she could.

Almost two hours had passed and they still wouldn't let her go home. Finally, they altered their interrogation tactics: "Ms. Sonya, there are three situations. A person can be a drug addict and get into a fight with someone; or a person has financial problems and owes money; or a person's wife commits adultery. In your husband's case, he doesn't take drugs and he doesn't drink. You are financially stable, so he doesn't have any financial problems. The last possibility is you are cheating on your husband."

Now they were very hard to my wife. They told her that out of three things the last one applies to her. They forced her to admit that she cheated on me with a guy named Jay. Sonya responded very calmly, "Look, they were my sister- in-law's brothers and her brothers were my brothers too. I had only one relationship with those three brothers, and that was only as sister."

In fact, those three brothers were her relatives in a way. They were third degree cousins. So Sonya told them that there is no way that I could get jealous and kill someone for that particular reason. We always had a good family relationship, and we helped those three brothers in every way we could to set them up in Philadelphia. Their apartment and their bills were under our name. They couldn't get anything due to a credit because they were new to this country. I had to do everything under my name.

Sonya was tired sitting on the chair for almost three hours. But those two detectives were now yelling at her and forcing her to admit the adulterous relationship. Sonya was crying while the two detectives repeatedly asked her why Shahil would do such a thing. Sonya responded: "We let you do every investigation you can. We didn't hide anything and we have told the truth. Why would you force me to tell a lie? What's the reason to harass me like this?" Finally, they decided to let her go home after they inquired about the date of the wedding. Sonya gave them exact date and time of the flight. They asked several times just to make sure that we are going to take same Plane. It was 9 p.m. at night. Since Sonya was pregnant and in pain, they decided to drop her off at home.

The two detectives were driving her home. They were driving fast. While they were driving, they were laughing and joking wrongfully too. Sonya, clearly felt that they were drunk. She was scared with their behavior. She also noticed the car was going on different route.

Sonya asked them as where they are taking her. They were still laughing and said, "don't worry, we will take you home." After half an hour drive, she came home and told me whatever happened in interview. I started to worry thinking they might destroy my plan to go back home to attend wedding.

That night Sonya couldn't sleep due to the pain from sitting for too long in the detective's office. As the pain wouldn't cease, I called the doctor's office. He advised me to bring her to the hospital as soon as possible. A couple of hours later she gave birth to Krish, my son, two weeks before the due date. Due to there non-stop harassments, Sonya went into labor early. But I thanked the Lord that both were perfectly ok.

Now, Sonya was at home for some months with Krish. The two detectives arrived at the house again after two months. Once, they picked up Krish and played with him. Sonya didn't like the fact that they were touching her son, but she couldn't say anything. They asked the same question: "When you are going home? When you are coming back?" We always told them the truth with the correct date and the correct time. In fact, my brother's family was also flying at the same time to attend the family wedding. There was nothing to hide about it. In fact, out of six detectives, four detectives told me "sorry to bother you, you are such a good family person" and returned my passport.

Only two mean detectives kept coming, I don't know why. As I have end up here in prison, they came to my house just on the night before the flight. When I asked them why they were arresting me they told me that "You may not come back and we want to put you on trial".

Shahil finished his story, looking straight into his lawyer's eyes. "Mr. Arthur, this is my story. I have done nothing. They have nothing against me, but they want to put me on trial anyway. They have crushed my wife's dream to go home to gather for the first time after my marriage. Shahil had tears in his eyes thinking about the case, time, money, and most of all the pain it will cause him from now on and most of all the reputation he had in his society would be destroyed too.

Mr. Phillip Arthur was in deep thought. If there is not enough to put someone on trial, there must be something else going on behind the scene. Either someone is jealous or someone is trying to trap him.

"Mr. Shahil, now that I know your part of the story, I must get a hold of the police record. First of all, I have to set up an appointment for the first hearing in court. I will try to get you out on bail first, and then we will take care of your case. I will have to see you a couple times. Don't worry," said Mr. Arthur when he left the place.

Shahil was alone for a few minutes. He realized that until the hearing, he had to stay in this kind of crappy place, away from home, Sonya, Suri and his handsome little buddy, Krish. He didn't know how long he would be away from his little prince.

8. Dr. Ashish at homeland

Dr. Ashish Mehra, Piyasi and their son were on the plane to go back home to attend the wedding. Piyasi was thinking about Sonya, who wouldn't be able to attend the wedding after all. She was preparing her mind as to what she would tell all the family members when they would inquire about Shahil. She told Sonya not to mention anything to anybody and just to say that Shahil had an accident. That way she could inform all the family members and relatives. She also talked to her husband as to what he should say to everyone. That would be very easy to get out from answering to everyone's question and should be same answer from her and her husband Dr. Ashish.

The plane arrived at the Sahara Airport in Bombay at 6.00 a.m. in the morning. In the waiting area, Piyasi expected to see a lot of family members to receive them. But, to her surprise, very few of them showed up. As she came near each family member, she knelt out of respect and then she hugged each of them. After formal meeting they started to walk towards the limousine. The family limousine took them to Dr. Ashish Mehra's town. During the ride, Dr Ashish and some family members talked, but none of them had a smile of happiness at their arrival. Everyone's eyes were looking for Shahil and his family. Most of all, everyone was eagerly waiting to see Shahil's little prince and to hold him tight. After all Shahil was the youngest and dearest of all the family members, and this time he was coming with his little prince. So everyone was curious to see him more than Dr. Ashish and his wife Piyasi, unfortunately Shahil wasn't able to come.

Piyasi was a beautiful, young-looking woman. Dr. Ashish Mehra had chosen to marry Piyasi, the daughter of one of the richest families in town. After her marriage, she joined Dr. Ashish's family. In only three months, she had to leave her country and go to America since her husband worked as a doctor in an American hospital. Within three months, she was in good and bad terms with some family members. They were kind to her as she was the new bride of the family, but they also noted that she was proud. If someone said something as a joke, she would take it seriously and wouldn't talk to anyone or she would walk away to another room. Every so often she would suspect that other family members were talking about her. Everybody came to know her nature so they would not talk to her as much as they wanted to. Once she moved to America, she barely communicated with her in-laws.

Every time she went to visit her in-laws, she would barely talk to them, staying in her room most of the time. But if Dr. Ashish Mehra was with his family, she would be with them all joking and laughing. In a way, she was two-faced. Even Dr. Ashish Mehra didn't know all of this, because she was always good to her husband; he had no reason to think ill of her. Dr. Ashish Mehra was very busy doctor, who didn't have a time to think otherwise.

On the first day, no one asked Dr. Ashish and Piyasi any questions about Shahil just to make them feel welcome after the long trip. The next day everybody was busy with the holy rituals for the wedding ceremony. A lot of preparations were made, as the groom was the only son of Shahil's eldest brother Roshan. Additionally, Shahil's family was one of the richest families in town, so they prepared for a big wedding ceremony. Orders were given to prepare beautiful canopy and to decorate the marriage hall as best as they could. The town's best catering service was ordered for three days. Special stalls were ordered for children's food. They could eat anything they would like. Every corner of the hall was decorated with a beautiful flower vase. Beautiful chandeliers were lighted up on the ceilings. Chairs were decorated and covered with fine cloth. After the holy rituals by the priest, the wedding ceremony was about to take place.

Shahil's brother Roshan was talking to several different people at the same time to check on several different things. But somehow, he was doing his duty for the sake to do it. The happiness on his face had disappeared, as Shahil couldn't come. He remembered talking to little Suri on the phone. Suri was telling him in her cute little voice, "Big Papa, I am going to dance in wedding parade". Suri was calling him "Big Papa" instead of uncle. As Shahil was raised by his brother Roshan, so he was like his papa. Shahil's father had passed away when he was only ten years old. Shahil's eldest brother and his wife raised all seven siblings. Everyone ended up getting married, and they all were settled nicely in their lives. Shahil was the last to get married and now he had two children, who were very dear to "Big Papa". As he remembered little Suri's words over the phone, his eyes filled with tears. Little Suri, who was like his grand-child, was not at the wedding. She would have been everyone's little princess going from one hand to another hand having so much fun. And what about Krish? He hadn't seen him yet, with the exception of some photographs. He also worried about Sonya as she was alone with her problems in a foreign country.

Everything was in place and the wedding ceremony began. Piyasi got prepared like it was her own wedding. The wedding started with the Sanskrit verses spoken by the priest in the world's oldest language. After the ritual, it was time for the oath in front of Lord Fire; the bride and the groom had to walk seven rounds. While this process was going on, other attendees were throwing flower petals on the couple. Shahil's brother Roshan was watching everything in a quiet manner. It didn't feel like a real wedding to him without his brother (son) Shahil?

Finally, wedding was over. Next day was a day of reception.

This was a wedding of Shahil's only nephew and Roshan's only son. Roshan and his family invited so many relatives from far away places. The final preparations for reception on the next day were made. The stage was decorated nicely with two beautiful chairs for the married couple. All the guests started to come. They congratulated the bride and the groom and placed a gift on the special table set for the gifts. They were looking at the stage and especially at the bride and groom. The bride, in particular, looked beautiful.

Dr. Ashish Mehra and Piyasi were going from one table to another introducing themselves to the different guests. Piyasi wore a beautiful dress and extravagant jewelry. As she was walking from one guest to the next, talking, laughing, and joking, her brother in law Roshan was watching her fake expressions. So many relatives had a same questions: "Why is Shahil not here"? What happened?" Piyasi was telling everybody that Shahil had an accident. Some guests even asked them why she wasn't with him since he was alone with his wife. Piyasi's answered, "Oh no, he is fine.

It's just a minor accident". In the guests' eyes, it was a shameful situation to leave Shahil alone and come here to enjoy the wedding.

Until now, Piyasi didn't know that her brother-in-law Roshan knew that Shahil was actually in prison. Despite Piyasi's advice, Sonya went ahead and told the truth to the one responsible head of the family, Roshan, her respectable brother-in-law. She didn't tell anything to anyone else, not even her own family members. While Piyasi was pretending everything was fine, Roshan's heart grew heavy and crying by heart without any tears for Shahil's situation. For one moment, Roshan felt like slapping her for lying and abandoning Shahil and Sonya to their fate. He remembered how he took care of each family member during terrible times, making sure nobody was left to his or her own devices. Everybody loved each family member dearly and always stayed together in the time of best and worst. But Piyasi wasn't like any of her family members; she was selfish and cold-hearted. After her marriage, she was expected to support the entire family through all kinds of joy and sorrow. Yet, she stuck to herself. Even Dr. Ashish wasn't as caring and lovable as he used to be before marriage.

The reception hall was filled with many guests. Dinner was served on the table, including a variety of dishes. Everyone enjoyed the food. After dinner, they prepared for the dance. Once the music began, they danced until late into the night. Slowly, each guest said good-bye to Roshan. They also told him to take care of Shahil, and to stop worrying.

After one week, Piyasi and Dr. Ashish got ready to leave for America again. Roshan and Dr. Ashish met privately at a town's nearby lake. They sat there until late evening and talked about Shahil. Roshan told him that he knew about Shahil's real situation. Dr. Ashish surprised that how he knew about this all and how he was quite about the fact all this time. Roshan made him aware of the fact that Sonya called him at the same night when Shahil was arrested. Dr. Ashish didn't say anything to him, but he got angry with Sonya, as he now looked like a fool in front of his respectable older brother. Dr. Ashish couldn't say much as he had to please Piyasi at the same time, but he promised to take care of Shahil and his family upon his return home. At late evening, Dr. Ashish and Roshan left the lake area to return to home. On the way, they made couple stops to see some of the friends as Dr. Ashish was leaving next day.

The next morning, Roshan and his wife woke up early. They called for the limousine. All the family members were there to say good-bye to Dr. Ashish and his family. Every one hugged each other, but no one was as happy as they should be. Their only concern was Shahil. Every one was saying one thing only: "Take care of Shahil, we miss him so much". No one knew the truth, as Roshan didn't tell anyone. Otherwise, they would have been crying hard to hear about their brother's worst situation of his would be fine and they would see him and his family soon.

Piyasi looked happy, as she thought no one knows about the truth and her success in making them fool during her stay at home. Dr. Ashish and his family took a seat in the limousine. As limousine started, everyone waved their hand to say good bye. Who knows when they will be back again? Although, Dr. Ashish used to take a trip to home occasionally or at least every two years. But who knows god's will, good luck or bad luck? Shahil couldn't come at family's wedding time....everybody was thinking.

Limousine arrived at the airport on time. Piyasi and Dr. Ashish joined in line to check out for luggage. After check out, they were able to get in to plane. After formal duty of the plane, plane started to fly to

California. Dr. Ashish was quiet and thinking about what his brother Roshan told him. Plane was flying on it's way to California...........

9. First hearing

Arthur negotiated an appointment for the first hearing, but he couldn't get one earlier than 15 days. He called Sonya to inform her of the date. She was surprised to hear that it took so long, she wanted hearing as early as possible. But to her surprise, it was after 15 days.

She said to the lawyer: "What! After 15 days? Why so late"? I want to bring my Shahil as soon as possible. Mr. Phillip said to her: "Look, Ms. Sonya, you are so lucky that you got an appointment in 15 days. In some cases, they wouldn't even get date until after six months. So, Please thank Lord, and pray for his release.

Sonya had no choice than to accept the date for first hearing. She was upset as she never had to live alone before; her loneliness was killing her. Most of all, she was totally dependent on Shahil. She had never driven a car before. She never paid any bills. She never took care of any problems around the house. And all of a sudden, she was responsible for everything, two children, Shahil's case, work and the entire house.

Suddenly, a dreadful thought crept up. What if Shahil won't get the bail for his release? Putting her hand over her forehead, she started to cry. She previously hadn't considered this as a possible outcome. In a state of anxiety, questions arose: How long would they be separated? What would happen in the court? What if he didn't win the case? A dizzy spell slowly crept over her body and she went to lay down for a while.

Some of Shahil's family friends called Sonya, but she never told them about her situation. Every time she lied to them saying that Shahil was not at home. Shahil, Sonya and their friends used to get together every so often. But after Shahil's imprisonment,

Sonya never invited anyone or told them about Shahil's situation. It was such a shameful situation in her community that she could not explain them how and why it happened. The mere thought of it depressed her.

Mr. Phillip Arthur was setting his priorities for Shahil's case. First, he planned to get the records from the court. After reviewing all the paperwork, he decided to hire private detectives. Everything had to be done in 15 days for the hearing. He acquired some information about the court's room no. and the judge's name. He checked his appointment book for other court hearings. Fortunately, he had only one hearing that week, so he could focus on Shahil's case.

Mr. Phillip Arthur went to the receptionist area at the Court Building. He introduced himself to the receptionist and showed his ID. He requested copies of the papers on Shahil Mehra. The receptionist told him to be seated, while she was getting the requested papers. He took a seat on the sofa waiting for the papers. His thoughts wandered off to Sonya. This young lady was alone and didn't know anything. Shahil and Sonya never hired a lawyer during their investigation. What a big mistake! She also knew nothing about the criminal justice system. After nine months of investigation, they finally hired him. If they had hired him right from the start, Shahil wouldn't be in this situation. After listening to Shahil's story, it looked like there is nothing against him, so what's the purpose of arresting him? Well, I will know after I get the papers from police record, he thought.

Receptionist came to him after half an hour and called him. "Sir, here are your copies of the record," she said. Mr. Phillip Arthur thanked her and left for his office.

Mr. Phillip Arthur arrived at his office and immediately got to work.

First of all, he checked Shahil's polygraph test. It was fine; he had told the truth. Then he was going through the police detective findings. It was written in the big bold letters:

"No Motive,

"No Weapon found" "No blood found" "No Fiber match"

"Tire does not match"

As Mr. Phillip was going further, he also discovered information about Jay's murder. Two young factory workers found Jay's body early in the morning near the railway tracks in the Kensington area of Philadelphia, in the vicinity of Jay's work place. They were going out to buy coffee. As they left the building, one of the workers saw a person bent over to drop something. They thought that this guy was dropping a trash bag near the building, so they called the guy. Yet, he disappeared. When they went to check near that place, they found the dead body and called police.

Now Mr. Phillip Arthur read the police interview with the two workers, the two eyewitnesses in this case. Eyewitness Allen said, "I can't tell anything about him, but he was a heavy-set guy. He wore a flannel shirt and hat." He was the one who sat on the passenger's seat and thus had a chance to observe the events unfolding. He also mentioned that the guy drove a blue, old Japanese car.

The other eyewitness, Mike, merely pointed out that "The person was bent over, so I couldn't tell how he looked like. I couldn't see him because I was driving at the same time."

There was no other evidence for the case. But the killer did leave an imprint of the tire. The police took a print of it, but it didn't match Shahil's car. Mr. Arthur wondered on what basis they were able to charge Shahil? The only unusual thing he discovered was that Mike altered his eyewitness account. Hence, Mr. Arthur sent his own private detectives to interrogate the witnesses. They made a surprising discovery. Allen told them that he was interviewed by two detectives several times within the last four months. Seeing a picture of Shahil, he was coerced to say that "This is the guy." They kept telling him that this was the guy, who exchanged his blue car for a new one. Allen responded, "Sir, I haven't seen this guy at all. He doesn't look like a heavy-set man, and his overall structure doesn't resemble what I saw at the time. I don't want to put an innocent person on trial. It wouldn't be fair to him and his family." As Allen didn't respond the way the two detectives wanted, so they got angry and twisted his hand. Nonetheless, his answer remained the same.

Arthur's private detectives noted that Mike had changed his story. When they inquired about the altered story, he didn't respond. His first statement said that he couldn't see the person as he was bent over. Later on, he recognized Shahil as the culprit. Mr. Arthur was intrigued by Mike's changed testimony. Taking particular note of it, he sent his private detectives out again to confront Allen with the news. This time around they learned that Mike was the son of politician, and he was on the waiting list to become a police officer. He wanted to get his foot into the door by helping the police detectives. Allen knew everything about his friend, Mike. He fed the detectives of the truth as he was against putting someone innocent on trial.

Allen also knew that after long time investigation, they couldn't find the killer. Due to the pressure from the victim's family to solve the case, the police detectives tried to match the description in order to close the file forever. He gave some additional information to Mr. Arthur's private detective. He told them that his work area was situated in one of the city's dangerous neighborhoods. They are used to see a dead body every often. It's just poor and bad area that life is not worth for a ring or some few dollars in the pocket.

After interviewing the eyewitnesses, Mr. Phillip Arthur had one more thing to do. He wanted to know about the broken down car that Shahil sold to the gas station employee. The two private detectives went to the gas station and interviewed the man for a while. They soon learned that the repair cost was not expensive at all. But Shahil immediately told the man at the gas station that he didn't want to spend too much money, since it was a very old car. Taking advantage of that situation, the man told him that it would cost $700. His plan was to keep the car and use the good parts for other repairs. The police detectives were constantly harassing him to testify against Shahil. As he grew tired, he admitted to the private detectives that he lied to Shahil about the repair cost.

Mr. Arthur thought, in that situation Shahil had no choice other than selling his car for free. Mr. Arthur realized that if the gas station employee had related the correct repair cost, Shahil would not have sold it and he wouldn't have been in this kind of trouble. How rude to cheat some one! Shahil's case was nothing but one of bad politics. Poor Shahil! His car failed and the AAA service had to move the car to the nearest gas station. And guess what? The mechanic lied for no particular reason but for his own benefit. People could be selfish for their own benefit but what a disaster could happen when someone can be trapped in to their bad politics.

Mr. Arthur put his both hand over his head holding together and spread his legs on the coffee table in a relaxing manner. He was still pondering the surprising findings. Why would the police detectives charge Shahil? What's Shahil's fault in this case? He recalled the interview with Shahil. It looked like Shahil was a nice man. He cooperated in every manner he could, but the easier he tried to make it for them, the harder they were on him. Shahil was also a new immigrant to this country and had no knowledge of the court and police system. So, he let them in every time they came into his house. Shahil should have hired a Lawyer at that time and prevented them from coming into his house.

But Shahil had only one thing in his mind that he hadn't committed a crime so why should he worry? He didn't have to worry since he had passed the lie detector test. There wasn't anything against him so why would they charge him? Thinking this all, Shahil didn't hire lawyer at that time.

However, Shahil didn't know that a person could be charged based on circumstantial evidence. It could be created out of air and one didn't need to prove it. Circumstantial evidence could be coincidence and thus might contain no truth at all. The longer he thought about Shahil, the more he worried about the case. What would happen to this respectable young man?

Mr. Arthur took all the case related notes to present the case at the first hearing. The next day he set up an appointment with Sonya to discuss aspects of the case.

10. Sonya and Aryan

Sonya was worried about the first hearing. She was walking round and round thinking about Shahil. She wasn't in to ease at all. It's been some few days since Shahil left.

Pacing in her bedroom, she heard Krish crying. It was his feeding time and Sonya wasn't paying attention to him. As she went to Krish with the milk bottle, she heard the phone ring.

"Hi, Ms. Sonya," a voice said.

"Hi, who is this?" Sonya said.

"It's Mr. Arthur."

"Oh hi, Mr. Arthur," Sonya said. She felt happy as she was expecting a phone call from him. Mr. Arthur told her to see him the next day in his office and she agreed.

It was almost nine o'clock at night. She was just about to go to sleep when she heard the doorbell ring. She wasn't expecting any one, but she hesitantly opened the door. To her surprise, it was Aryan, Piyasi's younger brother. Although her life was destroyed because of him, she nonetheless invited him in.

After entering the house, he said, "Sonya, I am very sorry to have given away Shahil's name. I wasn't meant to do any harm to you. I was just thinking of a formal investigation, that's all. But my sister, Piyasi, wanted to put him on trial. I know that you are like my sister, and Shahil had helped us lot in putting us up in Philadelphia. Shahil fully cooperated with the investigating officers, and I have no doubt about his innocence. But now the case is in the court and I want to help you. Tell me if I can do anything for you."

Sonya was quietly listening to him; she didn't want to talk to him. She was very upset that her own family members went this far without even thinking of consequences. Aryan told her that Detective Chuck kept coming to his apartment to force him testify in court, so they can strengthen the case against Shahil. Yet, he didn't agree.

Sonya asked him what the detectives forced him to say. Sonya was surprised and shocked to hear that they tried to get her for having affair with Jay. Her eyes wide, still in a state of disbelief she said, How can you use my name? "Shahil and I have helped you guys in every way we could, believing that our sister-in-law's brothers are like our own brothers. How could you put Shahil in such dreadful circumstances? Just because they want to find a motive doesn't mean that they can use my name. What kind of proof do they have to use my name? It's such a Shame." Avoiding eye-contact, Aryan silently agreed.

All of a sudden, Sonya remembered her appointment with Mr. Arthur. She thought for a moment and asked Aryan, "Would you come to my lawyer's office and repeat what you have just told me. That could really help the case." Aryan agreed to come to her lawyer's office and shortly thereafter left the house. Usually, if he came to Sonya's house, he would play with children, would spend some time with Shahil's family. But today he left without waiting long.

Sonya went into deep thought. How good was our relationship with these three brothers? In the eyes of his brother Dr. Ashish Mehra, Shahil was the most trustworthy person. When the three brothers first came to America, they lived with their sister Piyasi. They couldn't find a job in her town for quite some time. Then Dr. Ashish sent two brothers to Shahil's home in Philadelphia, thinking it would be a good place to find work. The youngest brother Aryan stayed with his sister for further education.

Shahil helped them to get a job by taking them from one office place to another. Both brothers found job in a few days. They both lived with Sonya & Shahil for about eight months. Shahil never charged a penny for room and board as he considered his sister-in-law's brothers as his own brothers. After eight months, both brothers had enough money to move into an apartment. Shahil helped them to buy every item they needed to live in a new home. He went from one furniture store to another to get the best choice of furniture. Jay drove with Shahil since the brothers hadn't bought a car yet. At one point Jay pointed out to Shahil that he owns quite an old car. Since he already had such a nice house and enough money saved, he suggested that Shahil should also buy a new car. Shahil told him that Sonya loved this car so much; he would drive it until the very end. After setting up their new apartment, Aryan also moved in with his two brothers. Shahil always had a good relationship with them. They used to get together for birthdays and for other party events.

Sonya also recalled the day the car failed, and Shahil first called his brother for advice. His brother Dr. Ashish advised him to buy a new car for many reasons. Shahil bought a new car, but now they see it as such a big issue. What a shame! What selfish people! When Jay didn't come home, the other two brothers called Shahil. If they had any doubts about our relationship, why they would call Shahil first? They had a lot of other friends, and Piyasi could get any help she needed for herself and her brothers. Shahil was her only brother-in-law and she knew how much Shahil respected her as sister-in-law. Shahil would drop anything to do and any job for Piyasi and his brother Dr. Ashish. But it was all over now.

Instead of going to sleep, Sonya was still sitting on the sofa thinking about her past. Krish slept quietly on her lap. Her thoughts went back to Shahil, his work, as well as her own government job; they both led very good lives. Through a friend as well as her brothers, Sonya knew what Piyasi thought of them. However, Sonya and Shahil never paid any attention to it as Piyasi had everything she needed or wanted in her life as Ashish, her husband, was a reputed doctor. Lately, however, Sonya noticed traces of jealousy.

Sonya and Shahil both had accounting job. A year ago, Shahil started a business, which wasn't profitable at all. But could they compare themselves with Dr. Ashish? Dr. Ashish was a specialist and his income level was way higher than their own. Piyasi should be happy with her life, but she became nonetheless jealous of the Mehras' happiness. As a result, Shahil had been charged with a terrible crime. Aryan told Sonya that Dr. Ashish didn't know anything about Piyasi's action, It was Piyasi, who wanted me to give Shahil's name. Dr. Ashish learned about it later on when Shahil called him. Sometime, in jealousy, one could get in to short thinking process and as a result, they can be in the wrong path. Sonya didn't recall ever disrespecting her sister-in-law Piyasi and brother-in-law Dr. Ashish. One thing she was aware of was that when Sonya got married, everyone in the family gossiped about Piyasi. She never paid any attention to it however, she always respected her sister-in-law Piyasi.

Sonya and Piyasi both were from the same town back home. In fact, Piyasi's family was related to Sonya's grandfather. They both grew up in the same environment of higher family values. It was a lifestyle that demanded no relationships with boys until marriage. Sonya followed that pattern along with her sisters and cousins. Sonya believed in inner good qualities over outer appearance. Sonya was a very smart but simple beautiful girl in college. Her name belonged to the list of good girls in town. Her grandfather and her uncles were one of the town's best people. Due to their family reputation and Sonya's reputation in the town, Shahil choose to marry Sonya.

Sonya viewed America as the land of opportunity and the land of freedom. She noticed that just because one lived in America, people started to think that they had all kinds of freedom: freedom of love, freedom of divorce, freedom of getting married many times, freedom of sex, freedom of this and freedom of that. Regardless, Sonya believed that moral values in life were very important. To live a life in a proper way was very important to her. She never had an affair in college, why she would have affair now after getting married to Shahil? Shahil was her heart. They had a fun life together. They had many friends. Sonya still couldn't shake the thought of being accused of adultery. She felt shame on thinking over what Aryan told her.

It was past midnight and Sonya was feeling sleepy now. Krish was still sleeping in her lap. Slowly, she took Krish in her hands, kissed his head and went to her bedroom. She put Krish into the crib, covered him properly with velvety teddy bear blanket, and went to sleep.

11. Hearing started

Taking off from work for a couple of hours, Sonya got up later than usual to go to the lawyer's office. After finishing her breakfast, she left for the office in center city Philadelphia. Mr. Phillip Arthur was waiting for her. He discussed the details uncovered by his private detectives. Specifically, he discussed the eyewitness reports and how one eyewitness had changed his story. He told her that there was nothing much in this case, so it was possible that the judge might reverse the charges and Shahil was free. There was also the possibility that since this was a first degree murder charge the case might go on trial even though there was no evidence. It would all depend on the judge and the city lawyers. Sonya didn't know much about court cases so she was listening quietly, but with a worried expression.

It pained her to hear about the charges. She argued with Mr. Arthur unable to understand how they could prosecute Shahil based on no evidence. Mr. Philip Arthur was uncomfortable as he felt unable to explain the situation to her. Then he addressed Sonya: "Look Ms. Sonya, you know your case and you are sure of your innocence. But the court hasn't heard anything yet. So, until that time and due to the nature of Jay's death, it has to be that kind of charges. As for the detectives, they perform their job just for the sake of doing their job and putting some one on trial. When they can't locate the perpetrator, they make sure they find someone to put on trial. The family pressure is too big; the family wants closure. I understand that in your case Shahil bought a new car for the right reason, but that's about it. I also know that the two detectives in charge lied to the District Attorney to get the arrest warrant for Shahil, by saying that Shahil may not come back. The fact is that it was just an excuse. Both Shahil and his brother were going back home and coming back here at the same time. Also, Shahil owned a passport for a long time. If he intended to run away, he would have done so by this time. So, what's purpose of lying? But now we have to deal with this bad situation, Ms. Sonya. Go home and pray for his release."

Sonya remembered to tell Mr. Arthur about Aryan's visit last night as well as his offer to help. Mr. Arthur was surprised to hear about the adultery charge. As there is no motive in this case, they are trying to fix one. Mr. Arthur suggested that Aryan should come in to sign a statement. He told her to stop by with him in a couple days. At the end, she left for her office in Center City.

At work, Sonya wasn't feeling good. Her mind was at the first hearing that would take place in a few days. She was worried about Shahil and the outcome. What if Shahil wouldn't get out on bail? The question kept spinning in her head and she wasn't able to pay any attention to her work. For the last couple days, she wasn't able to sleep, and her whole body was aching so much that it was very hard to sit on a chair for any extended period of time. She made so many mistakes in her project that her boss, Mr. Moskowitz, asked her if there was anything wrong with her. Sonya assured him that everything was fine, that she was just slightly worn out. She had no choice but to keep her mouth shut for her Shahil. Mr. Moskowitz didn't press the subject any further although he felt that Sonya was hiding something from him. He had known Sonya for last three years.

A few days passed by. Sonya was thinking of Dr. Ashish and Piyasi who were enjoying the wedding of their nephew; they should be back by now. Sonya wanted to call her brother-in-law, but she hesitated once the thought of Piyasi entered her mind. Her sister-in-law was a controlling woman. So far, Sonya hadn't even told her friends about Shahil. When their overseas trip was canceled, she just told her friends that little Krish was sick, and she was unable to travel long distance with her son. Thus, she avoided telling the truth to her friends. Now she didn't know how to tell her friends about Shahil's situation. As it was such a shameful situation in her society, what would her friends think of them? Everyone loved Shahil so much as he was a good friend and a nice person. How would everyone react after hearing the truth?

The night before the hearing, Sonya couldn't sleep at all. All night she was sitting on her bed, praying to her lord for Shahil's release. Early in the morning, her eyes closed for few minutes, but she had to wake up to go to court. It was very hard for her, as she couldn't sleep most night. Although she arrived there on time, Aryan never showed up. She thought he must have gotten busy with his college work and would at least show up for the first hearing.

It was her first court experience. She never told her friends about this matter, so no one was accompanying her. She reached the court building on time and found out the room no. on the 3rd floor. While she passed through the security system, she looked around for Aryan. But Aryan didn't show up at all. She became really angry. If Aryan didn't want to help than why had he came to her house? Why had he told her what transpired between him and detective? He didn't show up at the lawyer's office as he promised, and he didn't show up here, so what was the purpose of his late-night visit? Surely, his city lawyer or detective must have stopped him, as it was a very important matter to them. Finally, she was checked and passed through the security system and entered the courtroom. Her lawyer, Mr. Arthur, and the city lawyer were already present. They were waiting for the judge to take a seat and start the hearing.

The hearing began with the city lawyer explaining the situation as to why Mr. Shahil was in this case. As soon as he finished, Mr. Arthur started to speak up. After explaining Shahil's explanation, he presented the original statements from the two eyewitnesses and how it had been changed to a different statement. He also pointed out how the other eyewitness had been coerced to agree with the detectives.

Finally, Mr. Arthur said: "Judge, I have never seen a case in my life walk into the court room with no evidence and no motive at all. Absolutely, nothing at all. The charges should be reversed and my client should be set free."

The judge asked for a break; the verdict would come upon his return. Sonya was terribly worried and prayed to her Lord for Shahil's release. When the judge came back and announced his decision to set up identification through a line-up, as to present some more detail or evidence since there was nothing to decide with. Although, there was nothing held against Mr. Shahil at this time, he would be released on bail for $35,000.

Mr. Philip Arthur congratulated him for his release on bail, but he was also concerned about creating a line-up. Shahil was present in the court and he was allowed to see his lawyer. They discussed the matter; Shahil voiced his concern about his identity having been revealed to the eyewitness through the two detectives. The one eyewitness could easily identify him based upon the photograph. The result was very clear at the time, so Shahil told his lawyer that he was not ready for the line-up. Mr. Philip Arthur asked him how he intended to present the case.

Shahil had no other experience and Shahil had no one else to rely on for help. For a moment, he thought that Mr. Philip Arthur was getting greedy. If Shahil didn't agree with the line-up, there was nothing to present in court, and the case might be reversed by another assigned judge. This way, however, the lawyer wouldn't get his full fee. In fact, Shahil had a right to refuse the line-up. But Shahil had to do what his lawyer told him to do because he had to look out for his wife and his family. Where would Sonya go to find another lawyer? She would hardly find another one with no help. What about their children? Does she pay any attention on them? Shahil ultimately let Mr. Arthur do what he wanted to do. Maybe he knew more about this all. In the end, Shahil agreed to have a line up.

12. Collecting fund

Sonya was walking round and round in her bedroom thinking how to collect $35,000 for his release. She used the credit card up to the credit limit. Out of that, she gave $10,000 to Mr. Philip Arthur and kept some for bail. The rest of the money she had to get from friends. Shahil had some savings, but he used them all in his business investment. Unfortunately, the business was not profitable at all. So there wasn't much left for him. Now Sonya had no choice but to get help from her family friends. So far, they kept everything secret, but now what? She had to declare the truth. She was ashamed to discuss a matter like this and she didn't know how to start to talk about this to their friends. Finally, she decided that no matter what happens, she had to tell them, even if it ruptured the relationship. She was a member of the higher caste community and none of the members had been in this kind of situation before. Everybody was afraid of the police and the court system.

Finally, Sonya started to call some of her best friends. When someone picked up the phone, she first started to cry. She just couldn't talk to them at all, and she would hang up without talking. For Sonya, it was very troublesome to explain the situation, especially to one of Shahil's best friends. The second time, Sonya stopped herself from crying and encouraged herself to say something clearly. She called her friend Nikki and Nikki's husband Milan. Even though she spoke this time around, she couldn't stop crying: "Hello.....It's me,....S..o...n...y...a..."

Mr. Milan was on the phone. He said: Hi Sonya... what's up?

As Sonya didn't respond, he asked again: Sonya..... Sonya.....why don't you talk? Why are you crying? Is everything ok?

Finally Sonya said, "No Milan. Shahil is in trouble. Gently, Milan said, "Come on Sonya, you were crying like there was an earthquake. Just tell me what happened and we will help you. Do you want me to come to your house?" "Yes, if you can," she said. "Alright, I will be there in half an hour."

Sonya now tried to call a couple other friends in the same manner. Some of them were living far away and weren't able to come, so Sonya had no choice than to talk to them on the phone. She became courageous after she talked to Nikki and Milan. They were very surprised when Sonya told them the news. They just couldn't believe it. They were wondering if Shahil could commit such a crime. Why would he do that? They often got together on weekends and special occasions. Jay's family and Shahil's family were good friends. They were a happy couple. There must be some kind of mistake on behalf of the police department. They wanted to do whatever they could to save Shahil and his family; they told Sonya they would send them a check of the needed amount.

Sonya felt good that at least Milan and Nikki came to see her. It was a big burden on her for not talking to her friends about this matter due to the Shameful situation. Today, she decided to talk to them about each and every detail; her mind would be free from such a heavy burden. She was waiting for Nikki and Milan to come. She was not at ease; she looked outside the window every few minute or she would keep pacing in the room. She had to collect $35,000 from friends or Shahil wouldn't be able to come out on bail. She hoped for their help.

Finally, the doorbell rang. She was impatiently waiting for them so she just ran to the door to open it. As she welcomed them, she threw her face on Nikki's shoulder and cried. Nikki and Milan comforted her without saying a word. After some time, their first question was where is Shahil? Was there a car accident? Why was Shahil not here? They had many questions as Sonya hadn't been able to explain anything over the phone. Finally, Milan said, "Tell me Sonya, what happened? Why is Shahil in trouble?"

Teary-eyed, Sonya told them about Shahil's problem. As they were listening to her, with surprise, they couldn't believe anything that Sonya was telling them. They were in tears too while they were listening to her. They didn't know how to comfort Sonya in such a horrible moment. Their biggest question was: If Shahil had passed the lie- detector test, and there was no evidence against him, then why arrest him?

Why did the Police department wait so long to arrest him, since they knew about the selling of his car for months after Jay's death? They had been living in this country for so long. From watching daily news on TV, they knew that murder, rape and other violence were common in this society. But Milan never heard of anyone from his community to be involved in such a serious case. He belonged to such a wealthy community, that most of them were very well settled businessmen, doctors, engineers or consultants. They knew Shahil from his childhood, as they were from the same town back at their homeland. After the marriage both family became best friends. Their kids were born around same time. They also knew about his car situation, as they advised him many times to buy the house first and then a new car. Milan and Nikki were quiet for a moment and just nodded their heads for the incident was unbelievable. They wrote a check for a few thousands dollar to help Sonya and Shahil. They told her not to worry about returning this amount until they had enough for themselves. They asked Sonya if she wanted them to stay overnight. Sonya merely nodded yes. Then she said she would be grateful to them if they could stay overnight. They spend some time with the children too as they knew that in this condition, Sonya wasn't able to pay much attention to her children. They praised Krish as he becoming a big and handsome playful boy. On the next day after lunch, they said goodbye to Sonya. She thanked them for their help. They told Sonya to inform them about Shahil's return and to take care of herself and the children. Sonya promised them she would.

On their way to home, Nikki and Milan discussed the worst scenario for Shahil. No one knows when "Karma" brings troubled times. Sometimes it manifests itself through car accidents, sometimes hospital stays and sickness or even death. Such a happy family was in trouble all of a sudden. They thought about the good times they had with Shahil and Sonya. They used to get together every so often on weekends and for family occasions such as birthdays and anniversaries. They used to go on small vacation trips and special occasions together. They always had fun in each other's company. And now what was the situation? It was unbelievable to them. They went home and told the news to their family members. Nikki's mom was especially dear to Sonya. They were surprised to hear all this and felt sorry for Sonya. One after another, family members came to see Sonya and comforted her.

Sonya collected enough money for the bail from her good friends. She couldn't believe how lucky she was to have such good friends. Otherwise, with a limited credit how much would she be able to borrow from banks? And to bring Shahil home? He might have to stay until the case was over and that would be a long time. She thanked her Lord for the help and the good friends. She thought of the saying, "Friends in needs are friends indeed." She remembered written piece about friendship she used to read:

"Friendship is the comfort of knowing. There is always a shoulder to lean on,
a hand to reach out for,
and a heart to welcome home."

13. Shahil at home

As Sonya collected enough money for the bail, she went to a special office for Shahil's release. She handed the check to that cashier at the window.

The cashier gave her a release slip to take to the correctional facility. She went to that place, filled out some paper works, and handed the release slip. The officer told her that Mr. Shahil would be released in two days. She took a deep breath, looked up to the sky and thanked the Lord for any help he gave her and her family.

Two days later, Shahil came home by himself. Sonya wasn't able to drive the unknown route, so Shahil came by bus. As he came home, he hugged his two children and cried for a few minutes. He remembered that this was not the final thing. Nobody knew the outcome until the case would be over. What if he would be separated from his children? Within a few days, he felt alone without the children, and the children were alone without him. He stared at them for a few minutes, felt pity, cried again, and hugged them. He hugged Sonya too. In a couple days, all his friends came to see him one after another. Unlike before, Shahil didn't talk to them freely. Shahil felt Shameful to be in this kind of situation; his friends were not able to ask him anything either as they were also ashamed to ask any questions.

After Shahil came home, he sold his new brand car. Since the judge did not reverse his case, it had to go on until he would either win or lose. What about the lawyer's fees and what about the borrowed money? He had to work on paying off his debt.

Shahil and Sonya went to different car dealers to show their new brand car and get an estimate. To their surprise, they were able to get back no more than 50 % of the amount they had spent even though the car was only one year old. Shahil and Sonya were very upset to know that they spent so much money to buy their favorite car and now they had to sell it half price. They had no choice other than to sell their new car half price.

It was almost time for him to be ready for line-up. As instructed by his lawyer, he went to that place for line- up. He was very upset and he wasn't sure what he was doing. For the line-up, the lawyer told him to get some of his friend who looked like Shahil, but Shahil couldn't call anyone he knew as everybody was afraid of the police and the court. He tried to call one friend, but the he was afraid to be chosen and to get in trouble himself. Shahil didn't' get a chance to explain to him that even if he got picked, he wouldn't get in trouble. The line-up was just to prove that the eyewitness couldn't properly identify the perpetrator. Unfortunately, Shahil knew that he was going to be picked, as he knew that the two detectives had worked before with the eyewitness by showing his picture. Now that eyewitness had an idea of his face and features, he would easily identify him. Since he was one of the few people of another race, it would make it even easier.

Shahil was waiting for his lawyer. His lawyer came in a little late. He noticed the two detectives talking to the eyewitness. He also noticed that the two detectives signaled to each other and to the eyewitness, pointing at Shahil. He didn't understand what these two detectives were doing there. There shouldn't be anyone other than the city lawyer and the eyewitness. He was sure to be picked. Shahil was very upset that he had nobody to discuss this matter with and he had to agree with whatever his lawyer told him to do. He wasn't that long in this country, so it was hard for him to act on his own.

The line-up was created. There were two black guys, two white guys and Shahil. The lawyer was told that there would be some Indian guy in the line-up. But at the last minute, there was none. Now that Shahil was the only one, it was very easy to separate him from the other men. Finally, the one eyewitness who had changed his statement identified Shahil. The other eyewitness did not identify anyone as he felt coerced by the two detectives to pick Shahil. Unfortunately, for the case to go on trial even one eyewitness was enough. The two detectives had a smug smile on their faces, and shook hands. The lawyer decided to put in an appeal to cancel the line-up as it was not executed in a proper manner.

But the appeal was rejected; the line-up was credible as there were five people.

Mr. Arthur knew that the trial had to go on. Due to the photo identification, it was very easy for the eyewitness to identify Shahil. Otherwise, Shahil's case would have been reversed. Mr. Arthur called Shahil to know whether he wanted to have a jury or not. Shahil was from a different country, and they didn't have a jury system in his country's justice system. Unfamiliar with this process, Shahil told his lawyer to do whatever he needed to do.

Mr. Philip Arthur inquired about the judge. He had some experience with the one assigned to Shahil's case. Also, he knew that this judge was easy on the punishment. If Shahil won than there was nothing to worry, but if he lost than he would get a light punishment. He thought, jury process is long and boring and since there is nothing much against Shahil, why to spend so much time in Jury selection? He decided against a jury trial due to the lack of evidence against Shahil; a judge trial would be sufficient. Shahil could only acquiesce as he had no experience whatsoever. He had lots of friend, but he never approached them, as he was Shameful of this situation. His brother Ashish would have been able to advise him, but due to his wife Piyasi, Shahil never tried to contact him. Thus, judge trial was finalized after a couple months.

Mr. Arthur was preparing the case and trying to get additional evidence. He tried to contact the gas station mechanic, who had lied to Shahil about the car repair cost. He agreed to come. He also contacted the eyewitness, who was manipulated by the detectives, and he agreed to come to the court. Mr. Arthur also contacted Shahil's brother as a character witness. There were a couple other people present for character witness. Thus, Mr. Arthur prepared himself for the case to fight and win. Shahil's only hope was that he had taken the lie-detector test voluntarily, and had passed. He had nothing against him other than the one eyewitness who changed his story in retrospect; he hoped that his lawyer would be able to argue well. Shahil was waiting for the day to start the case in the court.

Meanwhile, Shahil decided to sell his business, which was not profitable ever since he bought it. He put his business on sale. But unfortunately, he couldn't get anybody for a long time to buy his business and when he got someone to buy it, he sold it for half the price he initially bought it. This way he lost money in his business too. He was a man and couldn't show his emotion but inside his heart; he was broke but he wasn't able to cry. He murmurs, "when hard luck comes, it brings all kind of problems at the same time." He lost money in business, he lost money with the new car, and he had to pay the lawyer's fees. Now that he sold his business, he had to look for a job. He passed examinations for a federal job, and he called for the interview too. Unfortunately, he had this charge on him, and he didn't get the federal job. He tried some private companies, and he finally found work. At this time, he had so much debt, that whatever Sonya and Shahil were earning, they had to pay off from their savings. If he lost the case, how would Sonya's work pay off the debt? It would be very hard for her with the two children. So, he tried to get another part-time job. He got some kind of contract work in the evening time with which Sonya could also help him.

Shahil started to work from morning to night. He hardly was able to spend time with his wife and children. Sonya also started to help him with his part-time job. One night, Sonya and Shahil were coming out of the building after work. They saw detective Chuck outside their building; he was hidden in the corner. Shahil noticed that he was still following him, but he acted like he hadn't seen the detective. Shahil told his wife: "Sonya, I don't understand why this detective is after me. I cooperate with him from day one. He didn't find anything against me other than that one eyewitness who was willing to come for his testimony. Now that the case is in the court, why is he still following me? Sonya, in one interview, that detective told me that "your wife is very pretty". Is he trying to follow you? We must be very careful." Shahil and Sonya were both very stressed due to the long work days so they let the discussion stop without giving much thought about it. Shahil saw tears in Sonya's eyes. Sonya said to him, "Shahil, what I am going to do if you lose the case. A single woman can get in trouble easily. I have had bad experiences with detective Chuck, and he is still following us. I am really scared." Shahil also seemed to be worried but didn't say anything.

Day after day Shahil worked hard to pay off some of his debt. He wanted to spend time with little Krish and Suri. But Shahil would leave early in the morning while Krish was still sleeping, and he would come home late night when Krish was already in bed. He hardly had time to see him playing. Krish was almost 11 months old, and he started to walk around the house. On Saturdays and Sundays, Shahil was off from his regular job, so he only had to work his part-time job. Those days he would get off late and go to work late. Krish was happy to see him around the house, and he wouldn't leave him for a minute. If Shahil had to go to work, he had to skip away from him, while Krish was playing with his toys. But as soon as Krish heard the garage door open, he would try to run after him. Instead of getting down step by step, he learned to slide down the steps so that he would be downstairs in the garage. He usually cried to go with Shahil.

One Saturday afternoon, Shahil and Sonya were both leaving for their part-time job. They tried to leave without Krish noticing them. Shahil opened the garage and he started the car. All of a sudden he remembered that he forgot something. He turned off the car and went upstairs to get his wallet. He didn't see Krish with his mom. He asked of Krish's whereabouts, but his mother pointed out that he must be playing in the other room. Shahil checked in the other room; Krish was not there either. Sonya was in the car waiting for Shahil. Shahil came downstairs and asked Sonya if she had seen Krish. Sonya said she hadn't seen him either. She got out of the car to check on Krish.

What she saw surprised her a lot. Krish was right behind the car intending to go with his parents. Sonya picked him up and started to cry. Looking at the sky, she said, "Oh my god, you saved him." He was right behind the car, but nobody had a clue. He was so little that Shahil and Sonya didn't even notice him walking behind the car. Sonya hugged him over and over and cried. What would have happened today if Shahil hadn't forgotten his wallet and hadn't stopped the car? Surely, Krish would have been crushed under the car. Krish was right behind the car and Shahil would have reversed the car without thinking for a minute. Today, God really blessed him by making Shahil forget something. Sonya looked at the sky over and over again to thank the Lord for saving little Krish's life. This was such a stressful time for Sonya and Shahil that both weren't able to pay attention to their children. Since then, they told Suri to watch over Krish and to hold Krish when they leave for work.

Shahil and Sonya were reminiscing about the past that night. Ever since this unfortunate thing happened in their life, they didn't have time to call or to get together with friends. Shahil used to play with Suri most evenings after work or take his children to the park, but for so many months they had no time for

Suri and Krish. This unfortunate event had ruined their beautiful and pleasant life. Four months passed by working hard day and night. Shahil was able to pay some of the money to one of his friends. He still had to work hard to pay most of his debt. He also kept checking on the case date that needed to be scheduled.

Mr. Arthur was still working on the case. Finally, Shahil got a phone call from his lawyer to inform him about the court date. It was just one month away. Shahil and Sonya were upset as they didn't know what would be next in their life. Granted, Shahil had some hope to win the case, as he didn't have anything against him; he was especially hopeful about his lie-detector test, which he took voluntarily and passed. This would be his first experience in the court. He didn't know anything about the process. Usually most case takes a few months or at least a few weeks to complete depending on the case. He was dependant on his lawyer as the lawyer had experience with criminal law practice. He decided to get together with his lawyer and discuss some of the points, especially about the mean detective, who was following them at late night. Would it make sense to talk about the small things? Shahil wasn't sure of anything anymore. He wasn't able to talk to his friends. He didn't want to invite anyone as everyone was afraid of the court and the police. Shahil and his community were family-oriented people than anything else. Naturally, they would be afraid of anything that was beyond their lifestyle limits. When friends came to see him, they would come without their children. And if they had to talk to family members about Shahil's matter, they would talk so slow that no one could hear. If someone entered the room, they would say "sh...sh...sh.....stop." They would watch the regular TV news, but they wouldn't see the murder and rape stories, as it had bad effects on their children and the house atmosphere. Hence, Shahil didn't want to invite any of his friends to listen to the case in court. But he decided to call a few friends just for character witness. The court case was scheduled on September 11, 1993 with Judge Alisa.

14. Shahil & Dr. Ashish

On September 10, Dr Ashish Mehra flew to Philadelphia for his brother's case. Shahil received him at the airport. They both were very upset that the family members were against each other. Dr. Ashish Mehra knew that Shahil wouldn't be capable of such a crime, and Shahil had a very good relationship with all three brothers. But unfortunately, his wife Piyasi and her brother Aryan went ahead to give Shahil's name just for the purpose of investigation. However, the detectives took the accusations seriously, especially since another family member was involved. As a result, they put him on trial. Dr. Ashish Mehra was for both parties – Piyasi's brother and his own brother Shahil. Of course, this put him in a very critical position.

Finally, Shahil opened his mouth and exclaimed: "Brother!" He threw his face on Dr. Ashish's shoulder and cried. He cried for a while thinking what will happen to his two little children and Sonya if he lose the case. After composing himself again, Shahil exclaimed: "Please tell the truth in court. I took your advice to buy a new car, and you told me not to waste a penny on the old car. Brother, you knew the situation of my car. To clear any of your doubts, I voluntarily took the lie-detector test and passed it. They thoroughly searched my car and nothing matched. What else can I do, Brother?" Dr. Ashish Mehra replied: "I will do my best, but Piyasi wants you to lose the case, because now she will look bad in our society. And due to my disabled daughter, Anna, I don't want to argue with her. If you have to go to jail for a few years, just go and finish everything. Shahil argued, "But Brother, what about my wife, my two children and me? How would I be able to live in our society after the prison term? I am innocent. Why am I paying the price? Why is Piyasi after me? I have always regarded her as my sister and mother. I supported the investigations for a long time. But she doesn't want to stop. What's wrong with her?"

Shahil remembered the day he discovered that Piyasi and her brother Aryan gave his name to the detectives as a suspect. He called Piyasi and said, "Sister, don't worry. If I were you, I would do the same. The deceased was your brother, and you loved him so much. You should investigate every one, even a family member. You can check anything you like." Shahil supported all kind of investigation from eight detectives and he was cleared of any doubt and was able to go back home.

15. Case start

On the morning of September 11, Sonya and Shahil went to the City Hall court building on the 4th floor. Passing through the security check, they were able to go to courtroom assigned for Shahil's case. Upon entering, they noticed that there was no one there other than the two guards and the typist, waiting for the judge and the lawyers. Within a few minutes, the two detectives entered and sat on the side. Shortly afterwards, Judge Alisa entered and took her seat on high chair, waiting for the two lawyers. It was very quiet inside the room. Shahil and Sonya were terribly afraid and uncomfortable in this atmosphere.

Detective Chuck got up and approached the judge. He started a little friendly chat with the judge. Upset and suspicious, Sonya was looking at the detective as he was talking to the judge. She saw that Detective Chuck pointed at her when he talked to the judge. Judge Alisa also looked at her as if she questioned something. Sonya didn't take long to understand what Detective Chuck was talking about. As she knew that there was no motif in this case, he was trying to create a motif based upon adultery. When she saw the detective pointing at her, she instantly understood that he was planting poisonous seeds into the judge's mind, which can create prejudicial result of the case. Growing more and more uneasy, Sonya left the room for a few minutes after pointing out the whole scenario to Shahil.

When she was out in the hallway, tears streamed down her face, thinking that detective chuck was planning to do his wrong before even case starts. She had heard that the judge personally never talks to anyone from either party until the case finishes. So, how come this judge talked to the detective? What were they talking about? She was an educated young girl, and she knew the effect of a prejudiced mind. Everyday hundreds of case they were dealing with. They knew how to work intelligently, to get the result they wanted. But innocent people like Shahil had no idea as what to do to get out of this situation. Otherwise, Shahil wouldn't surrender his passport or give the correct date to go back to India. And if Shahil hadn't given a correct date to visit his family, he wouldn't have been arrested. He could have hired the lawyer the first day, but he didn't, thinking he didn't do anything and he had nothing to worry about. The more he tried to follow the path of justice, the more he was in trouble. Sonya went to the rest room to wash her face. She didn't want Shahil to know that she was crying outside in the hallway.

About half an hour later, both lawyers showed up.

The Judge ordered to present their case. Both lawyers introduced themselves and once again presented the case. The judge asked whether there was any evidence. Both lawyers answered "No."

They introduced the first photo line-up; there were six photos. They consisted of three brothers, who looked alike, and who were only 12 to 15 months apart from each other. So, they looked alike. One of them, of course, was "Jay". The other four pictures showed the three brothers separately; one picture included Shahil with the three brothers. Looking at the photos, it was obvious that only Shahil looked different. Since a brother wouldn't kill his own brother, Shahil was selected in the first photo line-up.

Mr. Arthur objected, as Shahil's photo was obviously different from the rest. Judge Alisa agreed with Mr. Arthur and ordered to disregard the first line-up. Mr. Arthur considered this a good start.

The two detectives, however, had developed a different plan within a few minutes. They told the judge that there was a second photo identification after this. They showed another pair of photos, in which they arranged six different pictures from different racial groups. They were not alike at all. The eyewitness still selected Shahil, since he knew how Shahil looked like.

Judge passed the second photo identification. Mr. Arthur argued that it's not permissible since the person had already been identified in the first case. He requested to suspend the second photo identification. The judge explained that since the two photo line-ups were separate from each other, she was ok to permit to accept the second one as evidence. Mr. Arthur strongly disagreed with the judge's decision. He pointed out that anyone could select the same picture once it was registered in the mind. Nonetheless, Judge Alisa dismissed his argument.

The two detectives ran outside the courtroom as they won the first argument. They shook hands and laughed. Sonya had remained outside all this time and didn't know what was going on. Her observation at the detectives told her that the case went badly. She started pacing in the hallway impatiently, thinking what had happened.

After the introduction of the photo identification, the first day's hearing was over.

As they were leaving the court, Shahil had a meeting with Mr. Arthur. He explained that he was hopeful to win the case, but the approved second photo identification would create some problems. Mr. Arthur felt sorry for Shahil and his family. By now he knew Shahil's personal history and his background. He had fought hundreds of criminal cases, but he had never felt like this before. He put his hand on Shahil's back, told him to take it easy, and left the court building.

Aryan was there too. Piyasi didn't come to court as it was a matter of her in-law's family; she didn't want to look bad in her society. She called Aryan to find out every bit of news. Aryan and Shahil's eyes met, but Aryan couldn't look at Shahil out of guilt. Though upset, Shahil looked hopeful and strong.

16. Detective's trick

On the next day, September 12, Shahil and Sonya arrived at court right on time. Sonya couldn't' get the picture of the two detectives out of her mind having their thumbs up. She thought, what would be the mean detective's plan after talking to judge pointing at her and suggestive photo line up? She wasn't at ease. Judge Alisa, both lawyers and the detectives had arrived on time as well.

Mr. Arthur had one eye witness, Mr. Allen, and the city lawyer had a one eyewitness, Mr. Mike Wilson. Mr. Mike was called on the stand. He took the oath to tell the truth. As he had changed his first testimony, he was asked several different questions. Mr. Arthur asked him why he changed his initial testimony of "I don't know how he looked like because he was bent over." He also referred to Mike's goal to be a policeman and how he wanted to get credit to help police. As he was the driver, he didn't have a better chance to look at the view; it was quite obvious. In his first day statement, he told the police that the guy looked Hispanic and heavy-built. Mr. Mehra didn't look Hispanic or heavy-built. After the interrogation was over, Mr. Mike was told to be seated.

Mr. Allen was called on the stand. He was told to take the oath. Mr. Allen was asked what he had seen at the place. Both lawyers asked a few questions. He told the judge that he did not see this person, pointing at Mr. Shahil Mehra. He described that the person he saw was short, heavy built, and Hispanic. He also confessed that he was coerced by two detectives to select Shahil's picture. When he didn't support them, they twisted his hand and went away. He said that he did not want to put an innocent person in jail, so he decided to tell the truth despite the detectives' use of force. Mr. Allen was told to be seated. There were no more eyewitnesses.

After this, the car mechanic from the Getty's Gas Station was called on the stand. He explained that he lied to Mr. Mehra about the true expense of the repair costs. Mr. Mehra had said that if the expense was over $250, he would like to buy a new car. Taking advantage of this situation, he lied to Mr. Mehra, and claimed that the expense would be about $700. And he did. Days later, the detectives contacted him to search the car. No evidence was found. Yet, the detectives kept harassing him.

It was almost midday. There were six different detectives present. They all got on the stand, one after the other, and told the judge that Mr. Mehra was very cooperative throughout the investigation; they agreed to return his passport to him. There was no evidence to charge him with the crime.

Then the two principal detectives came on the stand. They had many different stories for the judge. Mr. Mehra wanted to give all the answers to their questions. After listening to some points, Mr. Mehra got upset and impatiently got up from his chair and said, "No, that's not true. He is lying, your Honor." The judge replied, "Mr. Mehra, you will be given the chance to take a stand." This happened three to four times. Every time Mr. Mehra was told to be seated;

he would given chance to speak up. Shahil couldn't wait for his turn. But Mr. Arthur told him not to say anything because he might be misunderstood due to his weak English. Finally, at the end of a long day the hearing finished.

On the third day, September 13, Shahil and Sonya were told to bring the children and the mother with them as she was going to be on the stand as a character witness. There were a couple other character witnesses to be on the stand; Dr. Ashish Mehra was to be among them.

Sonya's mother was called first. Since she wasn't able to speak English, they used a translator for her. She was asked about Shahil's whereabouts on the day of Jay's death. She told the court that Shahil woke up at about 8.00 am, gave his children a bath, and got ready to go to his store. The bank receipt was presented to the court as a proof of Shahil's deposit from store merchandise sales. There were no more questions for her.

The next character witness was Dr. Ashish Mehra. He was asked some questions about Shahil's character. Dr. Ashish Mehra told the court about the car and his advice to buy a new car. He also said that they were all supposed to go to the wedding back home, so Shahil wasn't going to run away. Finally, he confirmed the good and trustworthy nature of Shahil's character.

Sonya was called on the stand, she took the oath. she was very very nervous. She started to twist her hair. She was so nervous that she wasn't able to stand straight on the stand. She realized that being nervous will not make their case good. Both lawyers asked various questions to Sonya. In fact, Sonya wanted to discuss the detectives' behavior as well as other things, but without any questions, she wasn't able to do so. She tried to say something about detective's rude behavior, but she was told that only thing she should answer is what is being asked to her at that time. Following Sonya, some friends were on the stand as character witnesses. Finally, the judge asked for a break to get ready for the final arguments.

At about two o'clock in the afternoon, the hearing resumed. Mr. Arthur and the city lawyer were going to present their final argument. According to the court's rule, the defendant's lawyer got to present the final argument first.

Collecting himself, Mr. Arthur began: "Your Honor, this is a very unusual case. It's not every day you get surprised by bodies. Then the eyewitness started talking about people looking like hamburger. He was all over the parking lot, Your Honor, trying to answer the inconsistencies, trying to give a reason why on 5/25/92 he said, "he was bent over so I couldn't tell......" I didn't say it, I didn't write it, and I didn't sign the piece of paper.' He said it.

Now, if he is such a cool cucumber that he sees so many bodies a year...that's one more, who cares, I'm not excited. I'm not sure why he said that, but I submit to this court that this eyewitness presents mere nonsense.

Your Honor, this court must have some doubts in this case. I have been practicing law for 20 years, and I don't think I have ever seen the Commonwealth walk into the courtroom with no evidence at all in such a serious case. Nothing....absolutely nothing.......... Nothing scientific......... No motiv...... Nothing but one eyewitness who says an hour and a half after it happens:

"he was bent over so I couldn't tell what he looked like'."

The judge replied, "Right".

Mr. Arthur shaking his head: Nothing, judge nothing. Judge: "Right, you are absolutely right."

"Your Honor, how many Japanese cars run in this country? How many cars are blue? The witness is not sure about the car color either. The car's tire print does not match. Mr. Mehra was charged based upon the car he sold. Is that right? No, I don't think so. But those detectives couldn't find the right person, so after nine months they wanted to try him anyway. Just because he is on trial does not mean he is guilty. No, I don't think so. How many Asians have been killed? So many each year...And how many Asians have been found guilty? Almost none...

There are more Asians killed every day due to their wealth. They are hard-working businessmen and hard- working laborers. Mr. Jay was robbed to death in such a depressing area, where every day people are victimized. Mr. Mehra had no reason to rob him because he is wealthy enough. He also didn't have a terrible relationship with those three brothers. Mr. Mehra is a family-oriented, financially independent man. He has two beautiful children and a beautiful wife. He is unable to commit such a crime. And there is no motif, your Honor.

Your Honor, I request you to set him free.

Mr. Arthur finished his final argument. It was the city lawyer's turn to present his part of the argument.

The city lawyer started to argue over eyewitness. Since there was no other evidence against Mr. Mehra, he focused on how Mr. Jay was killed, how the weapon was used, and how many cuts there were in his body. And yet, there was no evidence at all. Mr. Mehra didn't do it, so he didn't use it. Someone else did it? By appealing to emotions, he kept repeating himself over and over again. He had almost doubt that he is loosing the case.

In the end he pointed out that Mr. Mehra tried to look good by presenting his nice looking family in the court.

Sonya heard it and started to cry.

It was three o'clock in the afternoon now and Judge Alisa retired for the final decision. Sonya was tense. Would Shahil be free today? What would happen to her and the children if Shahil were found guilty? She had her eyes closed and she prayed to the Lord. Tears were running down her cheeks; she held Shahil's hand.

Sonya's son had accompanied her as well. He was hungry and started to cry, but she didn't pay any attention to him.

After what seemed like an eternity to the Mehras, Judge Alisa reappeared and took a seat. As she began to speak, Sonya cried harder, praying to the Lord to protect Shahil and his family. Judge Alisa finished her introduction to the case and declared that Shahil was guilty of voluntary man slaughter, and sentenced to 5-10 years in prison.

As Sonya heard the verdict, she cried out loud: "No, Your Honor, this is not fair. Please say, you didn't say this." Judge Alisa responded: "Ms. Mehra, what are 5 to 10 years in prison?" Sonya broke down. Shahil had lost the case after all. Shahil cried like a child keeping his head on Mr. Arthur's shoulder. Everybody was surprised, as it was a first-degree murder case; it was reduced to fourth degree. There had to be something wrong.

Judge Alisa gave permission for an appeal within 15 days; otherwise Shahil would have to surrender in 15 days. Mr. Arthur told Shahil to see him next day in his office, as Shahil was not able to talk at this time. Aryan and Dr. Ashish Mehra were there too. Aryan appeared happy as his job to find a guilty person was over. Dr. Ashish Mehra had nothing to say, as he knew what his jealous wife and Aryan wanted from him. Shahil and Sonya drove home with their family. No one was able to talk on the way home. Sonya's face was red with tears; she didn't know what to do.

Friends also came along in order to comfort Shahil and Sonya.

As requested, Shahil and Sonya went to Mr. Arthur's office on the following day. Shahil wanted to appeal the judge's decision. Shahil and Sonya entered to the high-rise building and went to Mr. Arthur's office at 21st floor.

Mr. Arthur was waiting for them.

Mr. Arthur went straight to the point: "Have a seat, Mr. and Mrs. Mehra. I would like to discuss with you the appeal. You have to decide what to do. We must appeal within 15 days. My fees for the appeal would be $15,000." Shahil and Sonya were scared thinking what to do with extra fees. They both tried to explain the situation they were in and told Mr. Arthur that they could afford no more than $10,000. Mr. Arthur knew their financial situation, so he didn't argue about the fees and agreed to that amount.

Mr. Arthur explained that despite the appeal to the trial court, they were not going to win. The reason, "Judge Alisha, herself is going to review the case and she is not going to reverse her own judgement." The appeal was necessary to take the case to the higher court. Once the trial court denied the appeal, they would be able to go to the next level. Mr. Arthur's explanation surprised them. Sonya could only mutter in disbelief: "Oh, my God, what's the purpose of spending $10,000?" Mr. Arthur continued:

"Well, if you want to accept the judgment, Shahil must surrender himself within 15 days. Are you ready, Ms. Sonya?" Sonya's hands started to shake; with closed eyes she was picturing a future without Shahil.

Mr. Arthur also discussed the judge's impression in the entire court system. Most lawyers knew her as a "compromising Judge," and he showed them a newspaper article about the judge. She was the judge, who mostly tried to keep both parties happy. Sonya said: "But it's not fair. Why she would do that? If a person is innocent, it has to be "Not Guilty", it's not fair for either party. The true criminal is still roaming the street, committing more crimes and the innocent is spending his time away from his family."

"You are absolutely right, Ms. Mehra," sighed Mr. Arthur. "But Philadelphia is one of the cities with the highest crime rate. It has been surveyed that 80 % of true criminals are found, but what about the 20 %, which are not found? There are so many criminals that are street Romeos, who don't leave any identity traces behind. In that case, it just happens that some mismatch can put an innocent person on trial. In your case, Shahil passed the liar detective test. Unfortunately, the detectives found a way to keep the test result from the hearing. There is no evidence against Shahil other than the eyewitness who changed his statement."

Sonya also explained to Mr. Arthur how the detectives were pointing at her on the first day of the trial. He didn't know anything about this matter. He was surprised but kept quiet, and thus brushed it aside as something of no importance.

It was almost afternoon. Mr. Arthur had another appointment with a client and Shahil and Sonya had to leave for home. Shahil didn't understand why Mr. Arthur didn't pick a jury trial. But without any judicial experience, he had to rely upon the lawyer. Many "what ifs" whirred through his mind, but the mistakes had been made. Shahil looked at his sleeping wife and felt sorry for her future life without him. What about the children? How would they be raised? How would he explain it to them? He wiped his teary eyes.

17. Shahil at work

Shahil and Sonya worked hard to pay off their debt as much as possible. There wasn't any fun around the house anymore. Shahil and Sonya would only talk if necessary — no laughter, no fun with the children and the entire family. They used to invite their friends over almost every weekend. They stopped calling them, and since their friends were familiar with the Mehras' situation, they didn't bother them either.

Mr. Arthur read the whole case carefully and prepared an appeal to the court. Five months passed by quickly. Shahil was waiting for the hearing date for the appeal in the trial court. Finally, his lawyer called him with the necessary information. Shahil and Sonya wore professional suits on the day they went to court. They hoped for the best; Sonya kept praying to her Lord.

Judge Alisa read her statement and final decision to both lawyers. Her decision was as followed: "After reviewing the whole case, the trial court rejects the appeal. Mr. Shahil Mehra has 15 days to surrender and appear at the court at 10.00 am; he can finish his business within that time limit."

Shahil and Sonya's spirit were broken. As Mr. Arthur had warned them, the trial judge didn't change her original judgment. Mr. Arthur advised them to appeal at the higher court; it was their last chance to prove Shahil not guilty. Before they left the court, Mr. Arthur also advised them to hire a different lawyer for the appeal to the higher court, as he didn't take those cases. Mr. Arthur thanked them for using his services, and the told Sonya to see him anytime she needed help.

In the evening, Shahil and Sonya started to discuss certain matters of the house once they retired to their bedroom. Shahil told her that he would show her how to take care of the finances. They had been married for five years now, but Sonya was completely dependent on Shahil. Her main job was to take care of the household chores and to go to work. She didn't know how to do banking or how to take care of their financial situation. She never wrote a single check in her life. She had a driver's license, but she never drove a car anywhere. Shahil would take her everywhere, even to the grocery store or to the doctor's. Now that she had to live by herself, she would have to learn driving properly. Shahil was deeply worried about her. How was she going to take care of this house along with the children? How would the children be raised without proper attention? That night Shahil and Sonya fell asleep exhausted and stressed out.

The following day, Dr. Ashish Mehra paid them a formality visit. He told them to sell the house and to move to an apartment since they were in debt. But Sonya pointed out that her government job provided a good salary and she would be just fine. Dr. Ashish replied coolly, "Look, I am just giving you advice. Do whatever you want to do; it's your choice." After some formal talk, he left for his home in California. Ever since Shahil and Sonya bought a house, Piyasi had noticed changes around the house and was thinking how they can afford such a nice and beautiful house just in five years in America? Thinking about Piyasi's moments of jealousy, Sonya was now determined not to sell the house. She would pay all her debt little by little.

Sonya knew her in-law's family. Dr. Ashish Mehra had a kind nature and was very good to his family. When she got married, a nice family atmosphere reigned. Dr. Ashish made everybody laugh by joking around the house. Everybody had dinner together, and at nighttime they chatted and laughed late into the night. It was really a pleasant time and family atmosphere. change in Dr. Ashish Mehra. After all, daughters-in-law were not like your own daughters and sisters. Why would they be so caring and loving to other family members? This was happening to so many families in today's society. "I" and "me" was a big problem, nothing but egotism. It was a widespread phenomenon. Sonya took a deep breath and sighed, she wished she could have a loving and caring family, free of jealousy. Right now she was thinking of her own brothers and sisters, who were thousands mile far away in India. She wished to run there and cry with her family about her situation.

18. Home Office work

"Sonya.....Sonya," she heard the voice say. She woke up startled. It was Shahil; he wanted to show her all the paperwork. They had very little time together and she had to be aware of the entire financial situation. Besides, Shahil also wanted to show her how to repair small things around the house. She never held a hammer or nail. From now on she would have to handle everything by herself.

At first, Shahil took her to his office desk. He showed her all the bills, payments, and the history of loans from different banks. He explained the importance of the due dates. If she wouldn't pay the bill on time or even a day late, she would pay additional finance charges, which she couldn't afford. He also showed her a spreadsheet on the computer, which he used to keep the billing records etc. up to date. She learned about the checking and savings accounts in the bank. There was barely any money left for an emergency. While Sonya was trying to understand this financial situation, she wondered how stressed Shahil would be with no money in the bank. They used to have a remarkable savings account. Tears fell from her eyes onto the paper, and the ink started to spread. Shahil couldn't stop his tears, and he hugged Sonya so tightly as if they were never going to separate. Yet, they had no choice.

Next, Shahil took her all around the house. He pointed out all the important outlets and the valves to shut off in case of emergency. He provided a few phone numbers to call for an emergency repair. Shahil knew from experience that once in a while they would need to repair something around the house. He also contacted his car mechanic. He told him that he was going to be away for some time, so he should take care of his wife's car any time she would need to bring it in. Shahil took her to the garden. He showed her how to mow the lawn. This would be a heavy job for Sonya; it would be wise to hire somebody to do it but she couldn't afford it right now. She decided to be strong and work very hard for Shahil and her dear family. If she were in India, she would have a maid to work around the house, to clean the dishes and to mop the floor. But in this country, labor was so costly that even rich people could hardly afford to have maid in the house. When she was young girl, she hardly worked around the house. She felt sorry for herself; now she had to work hard all by herself.

One and a half year-old Krish was walking behind Shahil and Sonya as they were in the garden. Sonya saw him laughing and giggling as he was on the swing. Sonya pushed his swing for a while thinking how Krish would feel. Krish didn't know about the separation from his dad in a few days. Krish's habit was to go downstairs as soon as the automatic garage door would open. He would wait for his dad to get out of the car and pick him up in the air. He couldn't talk much yet, so he would have big questions and confusions as where is his dad and why he is not coming through his garage? He would definitely miss his dad. Suri was only five years old, but she had some idea that mom and dad were in some kind of trouble. She was nice and did anything she was told to do.

That night Shahil felt more relaxed, since he finished his task. After dinner, Sonya and Shahil retired to their bedroom early.

Softly, Sonya said: "Shahil, would you get mad at me if I say something to you?"

"No, why do you think I would get mad at you, sweetheart? I am dependent on you now. You have to take care of my two kids and the entire family." So Sonya asked, "Can we make a trip to Florida for one week?"

Shahil was surprised to hear this question.

"What? Are you crazy? You know our financial situation now. How can we afford to go anywhere? How can we go on vacation in such a time of depression?"

Sonya retorted: "Shahil, you know that even though we will fight for you in high court, we don't know what will happen. We are not sure when you will be back home and after how many years. It will be at least five years or maybe ten years if you don't win the case. Have you ever thought about our kids? When will you spend time together? Money is always a problem in life no matter how hard you work. If we keep thinking about money, we won't be able to enjoy anything in life. I am going to miss you so much and so will the kids. Why don't we borrow some more money on our credit card and I will work it off. I already have to pay so much; a couple thousand more do not matter at this point. Let's not make a big deal out of this. This will be a last chance for you to see our kids before they grow big. Please don't miss the chance to have fun with the kids." Amid tears, Sonya begged Shahil to agree.

Shahil was quiet for a while. He thought about where Sonya would be in the near future. Sonya was barely able to drive to the nearby grocery shops and malls after some driving practice with Shahil. Naturally, she wouldn't be able to drive long distance. She wouldn't be able to go to any vacation place for a long time. Also, she wouldn't feel better without her husband. For some religious occasions in the Hindu religion, a woman had to fast for her husband's better future and better life. In India, the occasion was called "Kadava Choth." Sonya had never missed. Shahil was sure that Sonya wouldn't enjoy anything on vacation without him. Also, for the past two years they had been in and out of court. They were not able to pay much attention to the kids. He pictured his two beautiful kids playing around the house, giggling, running, and jumping. They had no idea of mom and

145

dad's bad time. He thought about how much he was going to miss them and how much the kids were going to miss him. Sonya was right.

"Shahil," Sonya said, "are you awake?" Shahil nodded by saying "hummm." "What are you thinking?"

Shahil quickly turned to her and said, "Ok Sonya, we will go to Disney World. But we have to prepare as quick as possible. We have a total of fifteen days to finish all our business. Sonya got excited. Her biggest concern was the kid's happiness with their dad. They might remember being with their father one last time and how much fun they had together. She thought of videos and photographs to be taken of the kids. She thanked Lord and said good night to Shahil.

19. Visit to Florida

In the morning, Shahil and Sonya discussed renting a minivan, since they had a very old car. They started to pack clothes and other vacation supplies as quick as possible. They went to the store to buy children's clothes and other necessary items for their vacation. Shahil borrowed some more money on the credit card. They were going to leave early on the next day. When Suri heard about the news of Disney vacation, she got so excited that she started to jump in bed. Krish was still too young, so he didn't understand the excitement.

That night, Sonya asked Shahil: "Will you promise me something?

Shahil with an exclamation, What kind of promise, dear?

Promise me not to drive more than 65 MPH, no matter how long the drive will take." With a smile, Shahil replied: "Anything for you, dear."

Shahil recognized her worries at this time. Even though they were going on vacation, they were tense all the time. They were only going for the kids' happiness. Sonya knew that in such a bad time, Shahil would drive fast and would get into an accident. If it occurred, Sonya would be home alone with all the extra problems. Instead, she decided to drive slow and enjoy the scenic view all the way as much as possible.

The next day, Shahil and Sonya got up early in the morning, got ready and put the entire luggage in the back. She put Krish in his car seat. Suri took her place next to Krish. Sonya's mom had one full seat due to her age; that way she could lie down and rest. Finally, they left for Florida. As Shahil promised, he was driving right on speed limit. Sonya was quiet and watched the scenic view. They were not in the mood to have fun with the kids. They usually would play some games or sing songs with the kids. But this trip had a different mood. They just were trying to be together as an entire family for some time.

On the way, Shahil collected information about different places to enjoy. After two days of long driving, they arrived in Orlando, and rented a room in a reasonably cheap motel. They freshened up and rested before they began their fun vacation with the kids.

They went to Disney World, the EPCOT Center, Universal Studios and the water rides. Suri and Krish enjoyed the Disney rides; Suri was having fun dancing and singing songs with the Disney characters. They took lots of picture and recorded some events as well. They also visited places designed for kids. In a big park, they went to the Dinosaur land for kids. As Suri was in first grade, she was very interested in it. Shahil went with her and played for a couple hours. There was also an Aladdin parade in the park, which Suri enjoyed a lot. After five days, Shahil decided to leave Orlando. On the way home, he wanted to stop at the Miami Parrot Jungle and Miami Beach.

It took few hours to reach the Miami Parrot Jungle. It was a beautiful tropical jungle, where beautiful colorful parrots lived in open space. Suri got so excited to see the parrots walking free. She started to chase them. She fed them, and she held them on her hand, her shoulder and her head. Sonya took a lot of pictures and taped her as well. It was almost evening time, but Suri was still chasing after the parrots. She just didn't want to leave that place. When she was forced to leave Parrot Jungle, she cried for a while. Krish enjoyed his ride mostly in his stroller, for Sonya was afraid that he might get lost if she let him walk around freely. They stayed overnight at a motel. The following day they went to Miami Beach. Shahil and Suri had so much fun as they both loved the water. Sonya bought some souvenirs and gifts for her friends at work. Finally, they left for home. A week had gone by and the kids had such a good time and so much fun. Sonya wouldn't forget this time together with Shahil and the kids. The videos and the photographs would be her long time memory.

As they were returning back home, Shahil and Sonya, forgot their separation for a while. They enjoyed their time with the kids. They chatted, they sang and played games on the way home. Little Krish was singing a song in his cute broken words: "Rain… Rain….Go…away… come another day….Little Krish wants to play…..". Sonya looked at Krish and

Suri. They were so happy on their vacation to Disney World.

What would the kids ask her after their dad's departure? What was she going to tell them?

Shahil looked at her as she was in deep thought, and said, "Sonya, where are you, sweetheart? Come on, forget about everything and have some fun with us. After all, it was your wish to have a vacation together as a family. Now, have some fun." Sonya's eyes were filled with tears, but she didn't let Shahil know. She turned her face towards the window and said, "Look, it's such a beautiful scenic view." There was such a beautiful rain forest on both sides. Suri always loved the rain forest. If Suri could stop everybody, she would run in to forest to chase some deer and the birds. Sonya told Shahil to stop in order to take a short break. As Suri was getting out of the car, she saw a small crowd of deer among the trees. She got excited and tried to run after them, but Sonya and Shahil stopped her, as they didn't know much about wild life was in that place. They just stood there and took some pictures. They were so many of them. Sonya felt sorry for the deer as she had seen many accidents that killed deer. She had always loved deer as they were such beautiful and innocent animals. If she could, she would have kept them as a pet in her yard.

She remembered her childhood and the summer vacations, where she would go to her grandpa's house in a small town in India. In the morning, she would wake up hearing the beautiful voice of a Koo Koo bird on the mango tree from a nearby mango field, and there would be so many peacocks in the yard. Just like Suri she would run around to chase peacocks and feed them too. She would swing on the branches of the Banyan trees with lots of other girls. She would also visit a nearby river every evening with her girlfriends and try to cross the river. Whenever she came home with wet clothes, her grandpa would get angry and ground them for a couple days. At times, she would throw stones at the mango and other fruit trees to get fresh fruit and raw mango just for fun. She would ride on the horse buggy or the camel cart to go to a nearby market. It was such a beautiful and peaceful country life filled with fun; she missed it dearly after her marriage. Arriving in the United States, a modern life, with work, home, and family life became the order of the day. As any woman, she wanted to have all this, but she missed her beautiful, innocent and fun-filled childhood life without any stress.

After half an hour, Shahil asked Sonya: "Do you want to stay here or go home. It's time to go home, sweetheart, and you are just starring at this scenic view like you have never seen it before." Sonya, indeed, was lost in the past of her childhood life, but she kept silent. Suri was still watching the deer as they were coming and going. Shahil started the car and everybody had to leave that place. Sonya took a deep breath as she was leaving this beautiful place. While Shahil was driving, everybody fell asleep within half an hour. It was almost night time, and he was looking for a motel to stay overnight. On the way, he found a motel where he planned to stay. Shahil took a long bath to freshen up. They went for dinner, watched TV for a while, and slept. The next day they packed and headed home, hoping to reach home that night. Today would be the last day of their vacation.

After a two-day long drive, they finally reached their home. As Shahil opened his garage door, Sonya said, "Home, sweet home". Even though she had a nice vacation time, she missed home and home-cooked food. Sonya and Shahil took the bags out of the car. They unpacked their luggage and started to plan for the next day. There were only a few days left for Shahil with his family, and there was lot to do in those few days. Shahil was so tired of driving; he just wanted to rest for the day. But he was worried that Sonya still didn't know everything. Without resting, he started to look around the house and fixed many things. He showed some technicality to Sonya small problems around the house. He went over the paperwork and the deadlines again. He contacted all the best friends and invited them for dinner. Time was passing by fast.

20. The day to separate

There was only one day left. Sonya and Shahil were both very upset.

There was a long silence between them. They couldn't talk to each other. Shahil was thinking about what would happen to Sonya and kids. Sonya was wondering what would happen to Shahil without his family? How would she be able to take care of the house and the family? So far, she never did anything around the house other than cooking and cleaning. Now she had to manage everything as a businesswoman: in fact, she was just a housewife. Her body was aching as time was so close to separate from Shahil. She was also worried about Shahil. How would he live and eat? There wouldn't be any spicy Indian food as he always wanted at home. Sonya took Shahil's hand and held it tight tried to sleep as she never wanted him to leave. Tears kept running down her face all night long. Shahil wasn't able to say anything, as he knew that he was helpless in this situation. Finally, they both slept for a couple of hours holding hands.

The day had come. Sonya and Shahil got up on time. Shahil dressed to go to court. Suri and Krish were playing around the house, as they didn't know of his absence for a few years. Finally, around ten o'clock in the morning he was ready to leave. Shahil called Suri over. He hugged her so hard and cried loudly. He couldn't say anything for few minutes, but then he began: "Suri, Dad is going to work in a different country and I will be out of town for quite some time. Take care of little Krish and Mom. I will call you everyday." Suri started to cry too as her dad was leaving for another country. He hugged Suri as she was very dear to him. Then he hugged little Krish and kissed him. He cried looking at kids, but Krish didn't understand as he was only 20 months old. For a few minutes, he kept looking at Krish; he looked so handsome with his black curly hair and long big eyes with curly eye lashes. Shahil said, "I will miss my little prince," and cried again. Finally, Shahil knelt in front of his mother-in-law with respect as she was Sonya's only relative and the only person to take care of the kids. He told her to take care of her health. Sonya was going to leave him to court so they left for the court.

Within half an hour, they reached the court building in Philadelphia. Shahil and Sonya both went to an office where he had to surrender himself. The officer took care of the paperwork and took him to a different office. Sonya had a last chance to hug him and to say goodbye; she hugged him, and she knelt to touch his feet to pay respect as her husband. It was her way to say goodbye. She was kept starring at him until he disappeared from sight. Sonya sat down on a chair and cried for a while. What a bad luck she had to leave her dear hubby in this situation! Finally, she tried to go home. For the first time, she would be driving home by herself from Center City. It was May 1994.

21. First day home alone

Sonya was home alone with the two kids. She felt so different in and around the house without Shahil. For several days, she had the blues, and she couldn't do much for her children. She looked at them as if she didn't know them. She would hardly smile or talk to them. Sonya's mom knew the situation so she took care of little Krish and Suri without any concern. Sonya wouldn't eat properly the way she used to eat. Sonya's mom told her: "Whatever happened has happened, but you must take care of yourself and your kids. How long will you be upset? Come on now, get up and do something."

First time after Shahil left, she cried loudly and put her head on her mother's lap. Sonya said, "Mom, I just don't know what to do without Shahil. I feel like there is nothing without him in this world. I love him so much. How can I bring him back?" She cried for a while; she felt relief and light- hearted by letting her pain out of her chest. After so many days, she tried to eat. There were so many things to do after Shahil left, but she didn't even think of any of it.

Sonya had to see a new lawyer to take the appeal to the higher court. Sonya called a lawyer and made an appointment to see him the next morning. Sonya was afraid to see him. Now she had to explain the whole situation all over again. Would he believe the coincidence of this case? How she would convince him of Shahil's innocence? The City of Philadelphia had so many crimes a year that most lawyers would just represent the case and to receive their fees. Would this lawyer be kind enough to understand the whole situation or he would just go by law? Either way she had to see him.

She got up early to see the lawyer Mr. Queen. She told the receptionist that she had appointment with Mr. Tom Quinn. The receptionist gave her a pleasant smile and told her to take a seat. She kept staring at the wall. She was worried whether she would be able to explain things properly. A few minutes passed by until Mr. Queen called her into his office.

"Hello, Mrs. Mehra, my pleasure to meet you. What can I do for you?" Sonya shook hands with Mr. Tom Queen and tried to give him a pleasant smile, hiding her real problem. She tried to be as professional as she could. Sonya had already talked to him briefly when she contacted the lawyer at first, so now she wanted to talk to him in detail. Sonya told him that she wanted to take her case to the higher court. She asked his permission to have more time to explain the details. Mr. Queen laughed and said, "Certainly, you can take your time. All my clients do. How I am going to work if I don't have any details?" Sonya felt much better after hearing that. She took a deep breath and sighed before she started to talk.

She felt that the lawyer was courteous enough to be patient. She thought he must be an experienced lawyer. Sometimes it is necessary to understand another person's situation, and to take some time just to be nice and listen to that person. Sonya contacted a few lawyers before choosing him. Most lawyers acted as if they didn't have time at all. If they didn't listen now, how were they going to listen to her later and work hard on her case? She had several bad experiences with lawyers. One lawyer told her that he only took criminal cases. Then she found out that they only dealt with divorce cases. One lawyer took from her a thousand dollar deposit for her case until she found out that his expertise was mostly injury cases. So far, Sonya was inexperienced with this, so she had to be very careful. It was hard for her to work by herself in this competitive professional world, for she was mostly a housewife. But now she was preparing herself to be as professional as she could be.

Sonya started to tell the whole story from beginning to end. She began with how her husband was trapped in this case. She explained that so far, there was no evidence against him, and there was no motif at all. She also expressed her feelings that they made a mistake by not having a jury, as they were new in this country and new to the court system. By appealing to the higher court, she wanted to free Shahil, or at least request a new trial where she can have a jury and justice. She told him how one of the eyewitnesses was forced to give Shahil's name. And at last, she told him how the detective pointed at her in the courtroom and whispered to the judge.

She speculated that since there was nothing against Shahil, they intended to use her as a motive. She had seen the statue of the goddess of justice in the court. There was a bandage on the eyes of the goddess of justice. What did that really mean? God created such intelligent human beings no one had control over what they thought. No law could control what you thought inside your mind, even if you had an outline that you could only do this or that. Sometime it was just an emotion over something you didn't like. But that emotion could push you to make the wrong decision. Judge Alisa knew, based upon the written statements, that there was no motif and no proof in this case. Then what were the two detectives talking about when they pointed at her? Did they try to create their own story? Even Judge Alisa used that story without any proof. Did that emotional idea impair her judgment?

Sonya asked her lawyer, "Why were the two detectives pointing at me." "Ms. Sonya, it's very simple. This case has no motiv and they wanted to create a motiv. There have to have motiv unless the person is mentally retarded.

In fact, you are a very beautiful young lady," Mr. Queen said and looked her straight into her eyes. "It's easy to target you."

"So? I am a married woman and I love my husband. And...and....in my religion it's a sin to think of another person after marriage." Sonya looked innocently at Mr. Queen.

"While that may be true, those detectives don't depend upon your religious belief. Lawyers can do anything to win the case. In fact, I have won a case in which a guilty person proved to be innocent. And in your case, your innocent husband was proven guilty. It's all about evidences and stories...fake or real. In fact, you should stop worrying about people and your society since this is the reality." Sonya thanked him and left to go to work.

She was waiting for the bus. There were beautiful high-rise buildings all around. She was amazed to see the beautiful blue, black and brown glass buildings. Modern technologies were so amazing that modern constructions looks so different and beautiful than some of the older buildings. Most buildings had amazing art included in the modern construction, which made it even more beautiful. She always appreciated artwork in any area. She would love to be an architect and get the chance to create new designs. Sonya was also working in one of the beautiful high-rise buildings for the State government; her office building was right in center city. She thought how inconvenient it was for someone to commute from the suburbs to center city every often. It was very easy for her to take a break from work and go to see the lawyers. In fact, she made several appointments with several different lawyers, just to look for the right one. Most lawyers' offices would be in Center City. With two little kids and other responsibilities, it would be very hard for her to run from the suburbs to center city. While she was waiting for the bus, she looked up to the sky and thanked the Lord for giving her some conveniences.

22. Sonya's boss

S onya's boss, Mike Moskowitz, was upset with her. She was taking off from work quite often that it really amazed him. Mr. Moskowitz asked her if everything was ok and why she had to take off from work so frequently. Usually Sonya had perfect attendance, but for the last couple months she looked worried and upset as if something was wrong in her life. She didn't have a pretty smile on her face anymore. Mr. Mike wanted to ask her about her personal situation, but he didn't think it was appropriate to inquire about it.

In fact, he knew Sonya's husband, Shahil pretty well. Mr. Mike lived in the same neighborhood just a few miles away from where Sonya was living. One time his car failed, and Shahil gave him a ride from the train station to his home while he was there to pick up Sonya from the train station. On the way, Mike talked with Shahil for some time, and since than he had a good impression of Shahil. Since then they met several times; Mr. Mike enjoyed talking to Shahil.

This time Mr. Mike called Sonya in his office and talked to her. "Sorry Sonya, if you don't mind, can I ask you something?

"Sure", Sonya said.

"Is every thing ok with you and Shahil? Is everything ok with your family?" Sonya knew that her boss Mr. Mike would ask her some day. It'd been very hard for her to hide everything, especially her sadness over Shahil's situation for the past couple months. Even though Sonya was prepared to answer his question, she couldn't control herself. Tears emerged in her eyes before she answered. Mike pulled a tissue from his drawer. For a few moments she stopped, and she said, "Yes, Mike, my son is sick, and I have to take him to the doctor at a hospital in center city." Sonya clearly lied to him. Sonya felt so sorry she had to lie to him, but she had no choice. There wasn't any other way to explain her family situation to her boss.

"Oh! I am so sorry to hear that. Let me know if I can be helpful to you in any way," Mr. Mike said.

Sonya thanked him for the offer, and went back to her office. She felt terrible for having lied to Mr. Mike.

Sonya had been working with him for the last five years. Mr. Mike was a Budget Officer, and Sonya was his Budget Assistant. In those five years, Sonya learned his lifestyle and working habits. He was a religious Jew and a very honest person. He was very particular in his working style and habits. His etiquettes and manners were at the highest level. But he was perfect in almost every matter that other employees in the office would hate to take his suggestions and would not cooperate the way he wanted. But Sonya was a foreigner, and she wouldn't say no to anything and cooperate with almost everything. In fact, Mike promoted her as his budget assistant after looking at Sonya's serious work style and quick learning style.

Sonya remembered her time as an accounting clerk. When she came to America after her marriage, she was afraid she would have to start her career with a hard labor job due to language problem. Even doctors and architects would work as technicians and sometimes hold lower positions than that. Sonya was amazed with this kind of lifestyle. She was from the higher caste community, and in her country higher caste people wouldn't hold any low positions. Before her marriage, she used to work for one of the best nationalized banks. When she came to America, however, she had so much trouble with communication and understanding other people that for a couple months she couldn't get a job. She waited for the opportunity and worked part-time in a factory. One of her friends suggested taking a test for a government job; she did it and got the job as an accounting clerk.

After an interview, her supervisor told other employees that they would see a pretty young lady, who couldn't speak English very well. Sonya started to work in that office, but she would hardly talk to someone. Sonya's work was perfect and quick. She learned most of her work in a few weeks. A visitor would come to her office and sometime stare at her, as she looked so young, innocent and different than others. After a few months, she took a promotional test and within year or so, she got a promotion as an accountant. During this time period, she was well prepared and her English had improved.

In this new department, she was working under a supervisor, who was perfect in the work but not as aggressive as he should be in assigning more work. Sonya learned detailed accounting work, but as she was quick in numbers and math, she finished her work faster. Thus, she had a lot of free time on her hands. Since she wouldn't interact much with others due to a lack of professional language speaking style, she would read office materials or magazines in her free time.

Mr. Mike Moskowitz used to work in a nearby office and used to run from the commissioner's office to the director's office to his office for his important budget projects. He had two budget assistants, but he had a hard time to get the work done due to a lack of efficiency. He noticed that Sonya was reading magazines in her free time, so he decided to come to Sonya. He called Sonya in his office. Sonya was highly impressed with his position, so she was afraid that she might have done some mistake and he was calling her to warn her.

Sonya went to his office and said, "May I come in, Sir?"

Oh, that's nice of you to call me "Sir," Mr. Mike said. Sonya said, "Oh, I am sorry, I haven't forgot my old lifestyle to address employees in such high position with "Sir." Mr. Mike replied, "That's ok...I will take it for now. But next time call me by name. My name is Mike Moskowitz. It is my pleasure to meet you. I hope you know my name."

In her country, it would be too rude to call someone by name, especially, people of higher positions and teachers in schools and colleges. Sonya hadn't forgotten her lifestyle yet. She was still hesitating to call someone by name as she still considered it to be rude. At first, she would be afraid to shake hands freely because she was used to say "Namaste" by joining her two hands together. It was a way to greet someone. But now, she was a professional woman, and she learned a new lifestyle along the way. She was shy, but changed a lot within a couple years.

Mr. Mike said, "Sonya, I know that you get some free time sometimes. Would you mind helping me out in preparing my reports?" Sonya got confused as to what to say. Sonya agreed, but she was afraid that she won't be able to do this kind of work. It looked like very high level of work to her. But she couldn't say "no" to Mr. Mike. Since then Mike started to come to her, and gave her an assignment with a complicated math formula and a detailed analysis of budget reports. Mr. Mike would explain her work assignments one at a time. Sonya learned quickly and returned his work perfect and errorless. He was always looking for accurate information by preparing his reports in certain ways. In a month or so, Sonya worked independently on certain reports. Mr. Mike was amazed to see how a new person like Sonya could help him instead of his own two budget assistants. Mr. Mike's two budget assistants were old-fashioned, and they weren't adopting the new computer programs and new methods as they were supposed to.

Looking at Sonya's situation, her immediate boss, Mr. Miller, was afraid to lose this new accountant, Sonya. He also liked her work so much. He called her in his office and told her not to help anyone without his permission. Sonya was confused with this new situation and wondered how she would say "no" to Mr. Mike's work. When Mr. Mike came to her with a new assignment, Sonya told him what her immediate boss wanted her to do. Mr. Mike had no choice as he was not her immediate boss. In addition, he was also from a different division. Employees from one division shouldn't work for another division without their immediate boss's permission. Mike held a high-level position, and he used to take advantage of this to give extra work to some employees once in a while.

Mr. Mike was pleased with Sonya's errorless and accurate report and working style. He immediately decided to give a promotion to Sonya as budget assistant, but there was a problem with his own boss. Sonya was new to this field, and more than that she wasn't a fluent English speaker. An employee in that position should be fluent in English and highly professional as she had to work with commissioners, directors and other departmental chiefs for budget reports. Mr. Mike and his boss Budget Director, Mr. Frank McNeil, had a long meeting to discuss the possible promotion of Sonya as his assistant. Mr. Mike explained that he would train her every way he could. He had tired to work with some of the employees who were more interested in their rights than in working hard. This particularly happened in any government offices, where employees were protected by unions.

23. Mike Moskowitz

A year before, Mr. Mike saw Sonya working in another department, where he had to visit to sign some paperwork. He thought the new young lady was as cute as a delicate flower. When Sonya started to work for his department, he recognized her immediately. He took the opportunity to work with her. One thing Mr. Mike was pleased about was that she always dressed well. Ever since she had been promoted as an accountant, she was very conscious about her style. Most of the time, she wore unique and different dresses. A couple employees in her division commented that Sonya is too "dressy".

Sonya just tried to look simple but professional in her nice looking dresses. Mr. Mike requested a meeting with Sonya to discuss some aspects of the position requirements. Budget Director Mr. Frank McNeil called Sonya and Mike Moskowitz for a meeting. He was meeting Sonya for the first time.

"Hello, Ms. Sonya Mehra. Pleased to meet you." Sonya shook his hand and responded with the same greetings. Over the past year, Sonya had become pretty confident in talking, and yet she was afraid to talk to Budget Director Mr. Frank McNeil. His personality was awesome. He was a tall man, well mannered, and had a great personality. Mr. Frank spoke with Sonya and explained the functions of the Budget unit. He also explained the importance of deadlines and working late nights to finish the projects by the due dates. Sonya was quietly listening to him. In order to hear her voice, he asked her some questions. Sonya was pretty shy, but she tried her best to give satisfying answers. Mr. Frank was pleased but somewhat concerned as Sonya's ascent was different. Nonetheless, he thought it was a cute ascent. Sonya might have to attend almost all the meetings with Mr. Mike Moskowitz as a budget assistant. And sometimes, in case of Mr. Mike's absence, she might have to work on behalf of him too. While Mr. Frank McNeil was slightly concerned about it, Mike Moskowitz was very confident about Sonya and her work that he decided to promote her anyway.

Sonya started to work for Mike in the Fiscal Unit. Sonya learned to work with different kinds of reports and analysis. Sonya found Mr. Mike very tough when it came to honesty, integrity, etiquettes, and manners. Everything had to be perfect in his way, Once he said something, it had to be that way. There wasn't any free time for her as office hours were solely for work and not for fun or free time. Most of the work had to be finished in a timely manner. Sonya was getting used to it though. It was a chance for her to grow professionally and personally. It was going to make her the person she was meant to be.

In just four months, Mr. Mike had to go on vacation for 15 days. Mr. Frank McNeil was afraid to approve his vacation time, as the budget reports were due by the same time. Mike told Mr. Frank not to worry. If he had any questions, he should ask Sonya; she would be able to give him all the information. Mr. Frank wondered how in just four months she would know reports of about a hundred and fifty pages and its detail. He shook his head, but he gave his permission for vacation anyway. For a few days, he seemed to worry about a lot of things. He didn't feel like talking to Sonya, as she was a newly hired employee. He called Mr. Mike on vacation, but Mike gave him the same answer: "Contact Sonya, and don't worry". For a moment, he was very upset with Mr. Mike, but he had no choice and he called Sonya in his office. When Sonya came to his office, Mr. Frank was shaking his head and looked worried; he started to ask question after question about the reports' details.

Luckily, Sonya was able to explain almost all his questions at the same time. Mr. Mike amazed with her quick answer. He looked so happy and while he was on the phone with other people, he told them that he was lucky to have such a good staff that he had all the information available despite Mike's absence. He thanked Sonya for all the details she provided. He also thanked Mike for training her so well.

Sonya also felt good about providing answers to Mr. Frank's questions. She thanked the Lord for giving her the ability to learn the reports, and most of all she thanked Mr. Mike Moskowitz to train her so well. She would, definitely, in trouble if she wouldn't be able to answer Frank's questions. Mike used to tell him that putting numbers together was one thing, but reading numbers quite another. It had to make sense.

She had a lot of respect for Mr. Mike Moskowitz as her boss.

Mr. Frank McNeil couldn't believe that he had other staff members, who worked here for so many years, and weren't able to help him during Mike's absence. For Mr. Frank, there was nobody else but Mike who knew all the details. They had worked together all those years, sharing details and discussions. Ever since this moment, Mr. Frank McNeil had so much respect for Sonya that he tried to involve her in most of his meetings. By attending all the meetings and listening to all the chiefs and heads, she learned that talking is an art. Presidents had to read their speech in a proper manner or it created many of problems. A single wrong word could create different meanings. Sonya didn't have to talk in presence of Mr. Mike and Mr. Frank, so for the most part she would listen quietly and try to figure out the outcome of that Meeting. Whithin few years, she was promoted to Budget Analyst.

Sonya thought about how helpful Mike Moskowitz was to her and how Frank McNeil put his trust on her. Now, she became a career oriented young woman and good English speaker as well. After being familiar with Mike's honesty and integrity, Sonya had lied to him about her personal matter. She told him that her son was sick. How would she tell Mike about Shahil and the problems he had due to his own family? Sonya felt like telling him the truth, but sometimes in life, when situations were out of control, it was better to hide.

That day Sonya felt so guilty that she couldn't work and she passed most of her time reminiscing about the past. She went home quite upset and feeling sorry for herself.

24. Krish misses daddy

S onya arrived home later than usual. There were some electrical wire problems with one of the trains. Many people were waiting at the train station due to late trains. When the train finally came, Sonya couldn't get a seat and she had to stand for forty-five minutes. While standing, she thought the train had to be late today only, when she was tired and upset? After getting off at her train stop, she drove home fast.

She opened the garage door with the remote control. As soon as the door opened, she saw little Krish in the garage. If she hadn't been familiar with

Krish's habit to wait in the garage for his Daddy, she would have driven right over him. Little Krish couldn't say anything, but Sonya could see his puzzled expression as he was looking for his Dad. His eyes were wondering and he said in broken words, "Daddy…Daddy…" Sonya picked him up, hugged him, and said in a slow voice, "Daddy won't be here for you for a long time, sweetheart." She kissed and hugged him again and again as she felt sorry for him. Krish, who was almost two, started to speak up a little bit; he said, "Whel…is…daddy?" Sonya spoke to him using his vocabulary and intonation, "Daddy…is in the offich…" Sonya didn't want to tell him what he couldn't understand. She ran upstairs to her master bedroom, threw herself on the bed and cried for a while. How could she explain to little Krish that he would have to wait for a long time to see his dad, or to sit on his lap?

Sonya's mom called her for dinner. Sonya changed her into a casual dress. For the past few weeks, Sonya wasn't paying any attention to the house and she wasn't helping her mom with the household chores. She also wasn't paying any attention to Suri's homework. She thought, she shouldn't put all the weight on her mom as she was old and she wasn't able to take care of herself. It would be too much for her to take care of the children and the chores around the house. Now she decided to forget about everything and take care of her family. Her mom used to feed Krish, but today Sonya fed him and helped Suri with her homework. She put them in bed on time. Sonya used to sing lullabies for Krish, but for so many weeks, she didn't sing any songs for him. She started singing, "Hush little baby, don't say a word, Mamma's going to buy you a mocking bird."

Within a few minutes, Krish fell asleep. She told Suri a bedtime story and Suri fell asleep too. Sonya tried to sleep, but she couldn't. Ever since Shahil left the house, she was afraid to be alone in the bedroom. But she couldn't tell anyone. There was no one nearby, and she didn't want to bother any of her friends. Each night, she would hear some kind of creepy noise, as if someone was walking upstairs slowly. As soon as she heard the noise, she would get out of bed and turn on the lights. She wouldn't dare to go out of her room, but she would start to pray to her lord right on her bed. Once she didn't hear anything, she would go to sleep. For her, the Lord was the only guardian to save her.

Months passed by. Everyday, Sonya would get up at five in the morning. She would spend more time with her early morning prayers. She had set up a beautiful little temple in the corner of her master bedroom, where she prayed for Shahil and the safety of her family. She would express all her concerns to her Lord as if she was talking to the Lord. She even started to pray in the evening. It allowed her to feel safe and she became more confident living by herself. She was almost thirty years old and never lived by herself in this country or back home. She had a big family back home and many uncles and aunts visiting them all the time. She had no one else in this country other than her brother-in-law Dr. Ashish and his wife Piyasi, who was her enemy now.

Most evenings, when Sonya was in the kitchen preparing dinner and finishing kitchen chores, Shahil would take care of Suri's homework, and later play with Suri and Krish. Little Krish used to hide somewhere and Suri would find him. Sonya used to listen to their laughter and giggling as they played catch with each other. Even Sonya would join them to play hide and seek after kitchen chores were accomplished.

The atmosphere around the house had quieted down very much. Sonya had lots of responsibilities paying the bills on time, mowing the lawn, vacuuming around the house, buying groceries, doing laundry and so on. She hardly got some free time as her responsibility was doubled as a single parent. She would get tired at the end of the day and she had no time to play with the children. Not only that, she had to call her lawyer from time to time to know about the appeal. Most of the time she would be so stressed, thinking about the result and what would happen to Shahil.

One evening, Suri came into the kitchen. Suri said, "Mom, can you play with us?" Sonya said, "If I get some time, I will play with you." Sonya couldn't go for another hour or so. Suri came to her again and said, "Mom, now can you please play with us"? Sonya said, "Suri, why don't you finish your homework and read some book. I don't have much time. I still have some other things to do." But Suri had already finished her homework and didn't feel like reading a story. She kept nagging Sonya for a while.

Sonya was tense trying to finish all the chores and to pay her bills on time. She had to keep up with paying her credit card debts. This time Sonya got angry and she slapped Suri's face. Suri started to cry and went to her room. Little Krish also started to cry as he saw Suri crying. For some time, it was sad atmosphere as both kids cried. So far Sonya used to hear laughter and giggling as children would play together by themselves, but this time they wanted mom to play with them too as Dad used to play with them. They truly missed their dad.

Sonya felt terrible for slapping Suri's face. If Shahil knew this, he would definitely get mad at her. She had promised Shahil to take care of the children as best as she could, but not to hurt them. Shahil loved both children so much. They both felt a great affection for their father, but not so much for their mother.

Sonya sat on the sofa in the family room without turning on the TV. She cried and still felt sorry for herself. After all, she was living for the kids and they represented the only support for her. She loved them dearly, so she couldn't understand why she did it. She wondered if she could plan her personal work in a better way and share her free time with the children to make them happy. After all, they were just innocent children, who didn't know their past or their future. They just wanted to spend their time in happiness. Sonya decided to organize all her work in a way that she could have more free time to play with them.

Sonya went upstairs late at night and checked on Suri and Krish. She took both of them to her bedroom and put them in her king size bed. She put herself between Krish and Suri, embracing both of them. She kissed both kids several times. Ever since, she let the children sleep in bed with her.

Ever since that day, Sonya played with kids hide and seek and tag. They would even sing songs and dance too. While playing hide and seek, she would hide in a place so that little Krish could catch her first; he would giggle as he could easily catch her. She would try to lose most games to make them happy.

25. Anonymous Phone at Midnight

The neighbors noticed Shahil was not coming home, going out, or working outside the house. The next-door neighbor used to talk to Shahil all the time. When he inquired about Shahil's whereabouts, Sonya told him that he was out of the country. The couple told Sonya to call for any help she might need. As time passed by, other neighbors noticed it too. Some neighbors didn't bother to ask anything, as it was a personal matter, and they thought they might have divorced. Sonya didn't bother to talk to anyone, as she was very upset with her own problem.

It was quiet night, while she was sleeping in her bedroom, the phone rang in the middle of the night. She thought it would be a call from her family from back home. Mostly, she used to get phone calls from her family in the middle of the night due to the time difference. She woke up and picked up the phone.

"Hello, baby," a deep slow voice said.

Sonya wondered who this person is and hung up the phone. On the next day, the phone rang again. Sonya picked up the phone. "Hello, baby" said the same very thick slow voice over the phone. Sonya got so scared; she didn't know what to do. She hung up the phone, but she couldn't sleep all night. She thought someone must have been watching her, as she was a single parent now. What if someone will break the window and enter the house in the middle of the night? She got up from her bed and looked out the window to see if someone was in the backyard or hiding behind the trees. She couldn't see anyone, and she didn't dare to go downstairs to the basement or to the yard. She spent all night worrying what will happen next. She remembered the time with Shahil, when she never had to worry about anything. No one called in the middle of the night. She passed rest of the night anyway she could.

The phone rang again on the third day. Sonya had to pick up the phone, thinking it could be the family from back home. If it was, then she wanted to cry with a family member to comfort herself.

"Hello, baby, I am going to get you." The deep voice was more than scary now. This time Sonya started to scream. This time there had to be someone around the house who intended to break in. Her mom woke up too. She got scared and got high blood pressure.

Sonya dialed 911 quickly. As soon as the operator picked up the phone, she impatiently started to talk to her about the stranger's voice. She told them that she needed help right away as someone might be around the house. The operator told her that the police would be right there in a moment. In a few minutes, the police arrived, talked to her and wrote up a report. Then they checked all around the house. When they couldn't find anyone, they advised her to change the current phone number, as it would be the wisest idea. They also gave her a phone tracking number for incoming phones; in case something happened, it would be easy for their department to track the phone.

The next morning, Sonya requested the telephone company to change the phone number. She had a different phone number now. She had to let her friends know of the new phone number, but she got so scared of the midnight phone calls, that she didn't call any of her friends or relatives for about a week or so. She was trying to get over the recent event. She didn't get any midnight phone calls after changing the phone number.

One late evening, she was helping Suri with her homework when the door bell rang. She heard the bell, but she didn't want to open the door as it was late and she was pretty scared of the midnight phone calls. She heard the doorbell over and over again. Finally, she turned on the outside lights and opened the door slightly to look who it might be. She was surprised to see one of Shahil's friends, Milan, and smiled.

Sonya said, "Oh! What a pleasant surprise?"

"Of course, I have to surprise you, since I have no phone number. I kept trying to call you for the past week or so; a message said that your phone had been disconnected and there was no further information. I was worried about you, so I decided to visit you."

"Oh, I see," Sonya said.

Sonya explained about the midnight phone calls and how she had to change her phone number. She apologized for not letting anybody know of her new phone number. Milan spent some time with Shahil's family and left. After that, Sonya called all her friends to give them the new phone number. But, she couldn't stop worrying; as she afraid that the stranger might visit her house and she could be in trouble. She kept praying to the Lord for her and the children's protection. She thought that it was just the beginning of her problems after Shahil left, what would happen until Shahil be back home.

26. Missing Krish

It was warm and sunny day. It was the first summer after Shahil left. The kids were tired of the cold winter and feeling locked inside the house. They were excited to play outside with the kids from the neighborhood. They saw some kids playing with the water balloons. Sonya also prepared some water balloons for the kids to play with. Most kids had bikes, skates, and many other things. Suri asked for a bike and skating shoes, but Sonya wasn't able to buy anything yet as she had lots of debt. Sonya promised her that she would definitely buy those items by her next birthday. The past three years had been pretty hectic as she passed her time back and forth in court for Shahil's case. She couldn't pay much attention to her children's needs as they were both working all day to pay off the extra expenses.

As Sonya decided to spend more time with the kids, she started to take the kids to the playground every evening after dinner. She hadn't been aware of all the parks around her area, but she started to explore new areas as she became more familiar with the neighborhood. Previously, Shahil used to drive them around and Sonya enjoyed the ride for the most part. She wouldn't pay much attention to the directions. She just hated to drive. But now she wanted to take the kids to different parks to make them happy. Within a year or so, Sonya had become a confident woman as she became experienced with lots of problematic areas here and there. She became more organized in planning her time with the dual duties as a single parent. Especially, Suri was such an enthusiastic child. She wanted everything different than most other kids. She would force Sonya to go to the nearby creek in the wooded area, where she could chase birds and deer.

She loved to watch the bird's nest hanging over the tree; she would run after rabbits. She loved nature so much. Most kids her age would play with toys, but Suri had different interests.

Fortunately, Shahil and Sonya bought their first home in such a nice neighborhood, surrounded by a wooded area, a creek at the end of the street and much open space. The backyard of her house had many tall trees. The front of the house also had a row of beautiful trees. The street would look so beautiful in the spring, and especially in the fall when the trees would change colors. When Suri was around four or five years old, she used to escape from the house without telling her mom; she would come outside on the front terrace and stare at the birds going back and forth between the trees. Once, her next-door neighbor was surprised to see Suri under the tree observing the birds all afternoon without getting tired. Although Sonya was watching her from her window every few minutes, her neighbor told her son to check why Suri was outside under the tree. Her teenage son came outside and looked up at the tree. He climbed up the tree and found a bird's nest. A couple birds kept coming to feed the newborns. Sonya's neighbor was surprised to hear that and came to complement her on her cute daughter.

Krish was three year old and looked handsome with his black curly hair. The neighbors on either side liked Krish so much that every so often they would buy candy and small game packs for him. Krish was more attached to his grandma than his mom as his grandma used to babysit him everyday. Sonya's mom used to take him out for a walk every evening while Sonya tried to finish kitchen chores.

It was a beautiful evening. Sonya was watering plants in her backyard while Krish was on the swing set. She noticed that Krish walked behind her as she went from one plant to the next. All of a sudden, she noticed Krish was not in the yard. Sonya thought her mother must have taken him out on a walk. She didn't mind, as she knew the routine. Later that evening, her mom came back home and she didn't see Krish around the house. When she asked Sonya about Krish, Sonya got scared and she said that she thought he was with her. Sonya's mom said that she didn't take him with her today. Sonya said, "Oh my god, where could he be?"

She started to cry, and ran downstairs to the car to look for Krish on the street. As soon as she started the car, both neighbors exclaimed: "Relax, we will come with you." One neighbor said that her son had seen the police with a child walking in the street. He had to be around somewhere. One of the women went with her. They soon spotted the police coming toward them with a child. Sonya ran to him, and grabbed Krish and hugged him. Little Krish was also looking for his house, which he couldn't find on the street, as most houses were alike. Police told her that this child was walking in the street alone and crying. A woman saw him and thought he must be lost. Hence, she called the police. Instead of taking the child with them, the police and the woman walked around to locate the child's home. Sonya thanked the woman; she was one of the neighbors from across the street. The police took the report from Sonya and warned her to be careful with the children. Sonya realized that while she was watering plants, Krish must have seen his grandma going out for a walk. When he ran after her, she had already taken a left turn and he couldn't find her. Looking for grand ma he went another direction and got lost. She was scared of her own carelessness and hugged and kissed him several times. She thought if Shahil would know this, he would definitely get mad at her.

In the beginning, Shahil called Sonya almost every day. As she got used to living alone, she told him to call only a couple times a week to save money on the phone bill. Shahil would talk to his kids and he would get so excited to listen to their sweet voices that he would start to cry to see them. He was almost eight hundred miles away from home. Sonya was still an unskilled driver, so he didn't want Sonya to visit him just yet. In addition, the car was very old and wasn't good enough to drive long distance. Shahil was dying to see his dear Sonya, his little prince Krish and his little princess Suri. He loved them dearly. Shahil was happy that Sonya had a good job and she was able to take care of most of the things. But how he would know what Sonya was going thru. Sonya wouldn't and didn't tell him about weird mid night phone calls and lost Krish just not to make him worry.

27. Appeal with Mr. Quinn

Sonya called her lawyer Mr. Quinn to inquire about the progress of the appeal. Several times her lawyer told her to see him as he had some questions. She satisfied most of his questions so far. This time her lawyer told her that in a month or so he hoped for the good result. Sonya got excited and started to dream about Shahil being reunited with his family again. She dreamed that the charges had been reversed by the high court and that she had won the case. She also envisioned how her reputation in her own society would be restored, a society that was family-oriented and valued morals and ethics. She dreamed of taking a nice vacation with Shahil and the children.

She used to read a newspaper, in which she saw cases where the person was found not guilty after 15 years. She read about how the case was taken care of and the detectives' mistakes. In several cases, she read about carelessness on behalf of the police department and their staff. Why would they care? They had nothing to lose if someone lost the case and was separated from their family. In one newspaper, she read about famous Judge Alisa and her personality. It was a big article about her method, "a compromising way," and her personal life too. She was a divorced woman and they discussed her personal problems.

For a judge, who is divorced, what does she know about the morals of marriage life? In a case like Shahil's where a person should get capital punishment, she gives a minimum punishment, because there wasn't any motif or evidence and the detectives were too lazy or careless to find the right person, "a Street Romeo" who must be roaming free on the street. If they had morals and ethics, why would they lie and manipulate? Why would they wait a year to charge someone? Sonya was from a country, where they didn't have a jury system. She never heard of wrongdoings and carelessness in a case like Jay's. So, she trusted the world's best democratic country the same way as she would trust her own people too. As a result, Shahil was separated from her and the children.

For the past two days, Sonya felt her eyes twitching. She was afraid to think about the end result. What would it be? She had been waiting for so long for the result to free her Shahil. She wasn't superstitious, but when she was a little girl, she heard that when something happened, good or bad, certain body parts start twitching. Knowing this all, she was constantly praying to win the case. Once again she neglected her children. When she was at home, she would work quietly as if no one was around her. As previously, her mother would take care of the children.

Any time she felt depressed, she would go to her little temple in her master bedroom and pray there. She would talk to the lord every time she went there. The lord wouldn't talk to her, but she felt like she was getting something out of talking to the Lord. She had lived such a nice honest life until now. Why did she get separated from her husband?

She would ask herself many questions about life, and karma. Automatically, she would get answers through meditation and understanding. She learned to take any situation lightly and learned to face it. When she was afraid and all alone, she would chant a mantra her father had taught her when she was a little girl. It would keep her calm.

Two weeks later, she got a phone call from her lawyer with good news and bad news. Sonya was concerned about the bad news and could only wonder what the good news would be. She instantly made an appointment to see Mr. Quinn. When she met Mr. Quinn, he explained that the higher court hadn't reversed the charges, but they received a new hearing with the lower court judge. Sonya was quite upset to hear the news, but a new trial would give them the opportunity to select a jury this time.

Within a month, Mr. Quinn had a hearing with Judge Alisa. As Sonya feared, the judge didn't grant them a new trial. Sonya broke with judge Alisha's decision and felt sorry that she wasn't able to free Shahil. In the hearing, judge Alisha asked Sonya as what a big deal in five to ten years? Why would you spend so much time and money for your husband? To judge Alisha, it was just a little punishment and it wasn't worthwhile to give her a new trial as it would be waste of time. To Sonya, it was a great big deal for her to free Shahil and live good reputed life instead of living with the shame in her society. In fact, it was a matter of true justice and judge shouldn't be concerned of wasting money or time. Sonya decided to keep fighting for justice, even if she lost money.

Sonya and Mr. Quinn had a meeting after the hearing. Sonya asked him whether she should take it to the Supreme Court or not. Mr. Queen advised her against this move. He told her that most courts would take their decision based on what the lower court judge had submitted. They had to prove Shahil's innocence by providing new evidence. Mr. Quinn had a detailed study of the case and referred to the tire prints that didn't match with the tire trace found on the scene. He considered it as an important part of the case. In fact, Mr. Philip Arthur made a big mistake by not focusing on this piece of evidence. Mr. Quinn suggested that she hire another lawyer, who was specialist in that matter, and provided her with some names. Sonya thanked him for taking on the case.

Sonya made an appointment with several other lawyers. This time, she selected Mr. James Brown as a PCRA lawyer. He had to hire an auto specialist engineer and submit that report to the court, but it was a long process and it would take a long time. Sonya had to wait either way so she decided to go for it. She presented all the details and paperwork to Mr. Brown so he could start to work on the case.

28. Snow fall

It was one of the coldest winters they had experienced. Sonya heard the weather forecast predicting heavy snowfall of about 30 to 32 inches. She had never seen as much snow since she arrived in this country. Sonya and the kids were excited about all the snowfall. Suri couldn't wait to build a snowman and throw snowballs at Krish. Since Sonya wasn't able to give them a pleasant time due to her stressful situation, Sonya thought it would be a good time to take them out of the house to go sleighing. Due to the heavy snowfall, most government offices were closed for three days, and of course, the schools were closed too.

Sonya's house was built on a hill, so Krish and Suri could both enjoy sliding in the snow. Sonya took some photos and taped a video of that pleasant time. Sonya's mom was concerned about Krish catching a cold so she sent him in, but Suri still built her big snowman. She got some friends to play with her, throwing snowball at each other. After long time Sonya was relaxed to see children's laughter and enjoyed playing with them too.

The next morning everyone in the street started to shovel, but Sonya started to worry of shoveling the snow from her driveways and sidewalks. In fact, she had never worked outside of the house. It was too much work to take on by herself. Everyone was making mountain of the snow on their side yard cleaning his or her driveways and sidewalks. The neighbors knew that Sonya had never worked outside so they helped her to shovel the snow. But by the time she finished, her pain ached, and she took off for the rest of the day.

After the heavy snowfall, it was a cold but pleasant day. Sonya stepped onto the front porch. Sonya was surprised to see the crystals hanging over the tree leaves and even from the roofs. What a harmonious atmosphere! For a moment, she felt like she was in heaven. A beautiful white snow all around and a clear crystals hanging over the trees made her felt like a heaven. She fell in love with nature. She thought of the starry sky, the sun, the moon and the earth full of mountains, rivers, lakes and oceans. She always loved and wished to take vacation to see the natural places, but without Shahil it was impossible for her. She looked up into the sky, closed her eyes for a moment and imagined to be with Shahil in those places she loved.

After three days of mini vacation due to heavy snow fall, Sonya went back to work. The employees in the office weren't excited to work after those days of leisure time. Everyone talked about the weather, as usual. Sonya was in her office listening to her other co-workers outside. While Sonya's mind wandered, she heard a knock on her office door.

Mike Moskowitz, her boss, said, "Good Morning, Sonya."

"Good Morning," Sonya said.

"How were your days off?" he said.

"Wonderful with the kids, but I had to work hard." Sonya realized her mistake and said, "I mean, my husband and I had to work hard to shovel the snow." Sonya had to make sure that no one should know her personal matter.

"Don't you have a snow blower?" Mike said. Sonya was confused and said, "No, not yet." Hummmm..........you should get one, He said. Mike Moskowitz was a person who could start discussing any topic with people. He was a very intelligent and talkative person. Sonya had to work with him most of the day, so while they worked they chatted about a lot of different subjects as well. So, she got to know him very well. She knew his interest in old-fashioned music, drama plays, shows, readings, writings and many other areas. In fact, Sonya learned her writing skills from him too. If Sonya had write an official memo, he would change it several times, explaining the deep meaning of it, and how it would affect the reader. His writing skill was highly professional and he would expect the same from Sonya, even though he knew that Sonya was a bi-lingual person. He couldn't expect her to be as professional as he was. He would give books and magazines to her to read to get a better understanding and better vision. He trained Sonya very well in few years. Sonya also was very happy to learn new things. In fact, she thought that she was lucky to have a boss like him. Often, a boss and his employees would have problems getting along. Mike was an elderly person, so Sonya considered him as her godfather due to the many things she learned from him.

Mike said, "Well, I am here to tell you that we have a meeting at 10.00 am in Frank McNeil's office. Sonya said she'd be there. Sonya prepared for the meeting, took her notepad and went to Frank's office at 10.02 a.m. Mike and Frank were both waiting for her. Frank was very particular about time, so he said in a joking mode: "Sonya, you are two minutes late".

Sonya smiled without saying anything and took her seat at the round fancy but old fashioned conference table. Frank started to talk in his usual manner, "Guess, what? We have a budget call.

Are you guys excited?"

Sonya knew that meant a time period of hard work, even weekends and late nights. It was a time to run around upstairs and downstairs from one division head to another division head getting all the information together and putting it together in a report form of one hundred and fifty pages. It would be very exciting but tiresome too. This time of the year was always a challenge.

He talked about preparing the annual budget and submitting it on time. He explained that there were many changes this time, so it would take much longer than usual and nobody would be allowed to take a vacation day off. They all had to work weekends and late nights; no one would be excused.

Looking at Sonya, he said, "Sonya, are you ok with this? You look serious about this."

In fact, Sonya worried about getting home on time and checking the kids' homework as well as taking care of many other things in Shahil's absence. But Sonya faintly smiled and said, "Oh, no…I am fine with everything." She had to hide her problems. For her, it would be another challenge to finish other things at home in a timely manner after the late hours at work.

Frank said, "I know, I can trust you," and laughed. Mike and Sonya laughed too. After the meeting, Sonya and Mike went to Mike's office to plan their work and time.

29. Car failed

Sonya used to go to work using the express train to Center City. Many times she considered driving on the Expressway. However, she wasn't a good driver and parking was a problem in crowded downtown as well. During rush hour, people would drive like crazy. She had heard of many accidents on highways due to rush hour traffic. She couldn't even imagine what would happen if she had an accident. Especially, what could happen to her kids and old mother who even couldn't speak the English. To avoid that entire situation, she chose to take a faster train. To take the train, she had to drive to the nearest train station a couple miles from her home. She would park her car on the station's parking lot. She had a very old car, but she hadn't had a problem so far.

She started to work on her project with confidence. She tried to work as fast as she could, so she could get home in a timely manner, but it wasn't only up to her. She had to rely on many other chiefs and heads to provide data. Once the information was available, everything had to be checked by Frank and Mike so she could use it in the report. One mistake could lead to several other mistakes due to complicated computer formulas.

After a couple days, Mike wanted her to work overtime. Sonya worked that day until late evening. After seven o'clock at night, the downtown area could be a scary place. Most office buildings were closed by that time and most employees went home by 5 or 6 o'clock. If you walked alone, you were more chances to get robbed. Sometimes gunshots could be heard. Sonya was afraid to leave by herself so she went home along with Mike Moskowitz, as he was also living in the same neighborhood. Mike was taking the same train and getting off one station before Sonya's. That night after getting off the train,

Sonya started her car, but it wouldn't. She checked many different things in her car, but she wasn't sure of what was wrong. As she was a member of AAA, the emergency roadside assistance, she decided to call them. Sonya thought about calling home too.

Since she had no cell phone, she went to the nearest telephone booth, called AAA emergency road service and called home but the home phone was busy. She knew that her mom would be worried sick, and that Suri wouldn't sleep without her. She thought it would be faster to get help from a passing car, so she started to wave her hand for help, but unfortunately, nobody stopped. After waiting for an hour, an auto mechanic from that company showed up. Sonya was eagerly waiting for the person, so she waved her hand as soon as she saw the van with the company's name. The mechanic checked her car and told her that her car's battery was dead due to the cold, and she should replace the battery as soon as possible. Finally, her car got fixed and she went home.

When she came home, her mom and Suri were crying as they were worried about Sonya's whereabouts. Her mom tried to call at work but no one picked up the phone. As she wasn't able to speak English, she couldn't even talk to her good neighbors.

Sonya's mom kept asking her why she was late and why she couldn't call. Sonya was so worn out that she wasn't able to speak up. For a few minutes, she sat down on the floor with her hands over the head and cried. Once she calmed down, she explained the situation to her mom. Sonya was very hungry but didn't feel to eat, so she went straight to bed.

30. Walking home at late night

While she tried to fall asleep, she thought about taking the car in for repairs. She didn't know where to take her car, how much it would cost and how much time the auto mechanic would take. She hadn't completely paid off the family debt, so she didn't want to spend too much money. She would be coming late for the next few days, so she had to figure out an alternative way to get home. Since the car was too old, she had to fix the car. She quickly decided to go to the train station by bus. She, then, got off from the bed, went to her office bag looking for the bus schedule, checked the schedule for the earliest and the latest ride. She went back to her bed to sleep. She wondered what if, in case, she would miss the last bus. After some thinking, she planned out that too as what to do.

As planned, she now went to the train station by bus. She came home by the latest bus she could take. Initially everything went well. Her mom, Suri and Krish were happy to see her on time.

The deadline at work was so close that they had to finish all the work by that time. Otherwise, Mike, Frank and Sonya would be held responsible by the Commissioner. Mike and Sonya executed the final check on all the reports that had to be submitted. As usual, Mike was very particular about all the details; he verified each line and each column to make sure everything was correct. He was so intent on doing his work right that it was almost ten o'clock and he kept working without paying attention to time. He almost got sick. His voice was thick and sick. But that was Mike Moskowitz; he worked with precision, no matter what.

Sonya was worried about her last bus from the train station. Sonya reminded Mike about the time to catch the train. Mike, it's ten thirty....Mike it's eleven......

Suri, on the other hand, would keep calling her, "Mom, when you going to be at home?" Sonya said to him, "Let's go Mike. We continue tomorrow." Sonya told Mike couple more times as she was worrying to go home by herself at late night. Mike said to her in his usual way, "why you worry so much? Your husband would take care of the children.....don't worry... Sonya....and he shook his head.

As Sonya couldn't explain her situation that she didn't have a car, she preferred to be quiet on that matter. She could have asked him for a ride home, but his first question would be "where is your husband?" She had already lied to him, and she didn't want to tell any more lies. So, she didn't say anything and waited to leave the office as soon as possible.

Finally, it was eleven o'clock and the last train was at 11.20 p.m. That day they took the last train to go home. Mike got off at his train station, thinking Sonya was safe as she had a car or her husband would pick her up. When she reached the train station, it was almost 12.05 a.m. She had missed the last bus at 11.40 p.m. She knew Mike and his working style; she had to work along with him and couldn't argue much. After all, she got her promotion due to Mike, and it was very helpful to her in her bad financial situation. She could have called a friend, but getting help one time.....two time ....and three time..... was ok, but getting help every often was not ok unless it would be life and death situation. She had already asked for help many times. As long as she could help herself, she decided to deal with the situation.

She got off the train which was almost empty accept couple passengers. It was a ....c....o....l....d.....and.....d...a....r....k.... night. There wasn't anyone at the train station except herself. As she had planned, she hid under a tree and checked her surroundings. There wasn't anyone there so she took out her husband's leather jacket from the bag she was carrying, and put it over her own ladies jacket. She made sure that she looked big like a man with double winter coat. She put on a hat and pushed her black curly hair underneath it. She also wore a scarf and her husband's gloves. Lastly, she hid the ladies purse under the jacket; that way no one would notice that a woman, at late night, was walking alone on the road. Sonya put her both hands in the pocket like a man and started to walk.

The train station was two miles away from her home. If she had to drive, the driving distance was about five minutes. But to walk it, it would take her at least forty to forty five minutes. She was living in a suburban area, so there were more trees and narrow roads. She had to cut good forty five minutes distance by walking as fast as she could. While she was walking, she was looking back and front, left and right to make sure nobody followed her. A few cars pass by. She thought, "Not everybody is bad, but who knows what may happen?" While walking, she chanted a mantra, her father gave it to her when she was little girl. She felt like she was protected by an angel, and an angle was walking with her too. She had almost walked half the distance, she saw car stopped by.

He said, "Miss, do you want a ride?" Sonya was scared to hear the voice. Sonya controlled herself, and said: "Oh no, here is my house". She quickly turned into the nearest street.

Sonya thought, how the man had recognized her? She made every attempt to look like a man, walking on the road. She checked her around. Her purse had given her away as it showed from underneath the leather jacket. She thought, no matter how much you try to be careful, there would always be something. She fixed herself.

When the car disappeared, she started to walk again. She wore two winter jackets and she was walking fast too, so she was sweating even in the cold weather. Finally, she reached home at around one o'clock at night. She stopped at the front steps, took a deep breath and said, "Home, sweet home. Thanks Lord for the help."

She rung the door bell. Her mom almost crying, hugged her when she opened the door. Suri was still watching a kid's movie, as she wouldn't sleep without her mom. After dinner, Sonya went to sleep with her two kids keeping them side by side, so.....dear to her.

31. Suri missing

It was spring season. Flowers were blooming with beautiful rosy pink and yellow colors. Trees were getting buds and green leaves. The spring weather was so beautiful that Sonya wanted to escape from the house. Usually, when Shahil was with her, they used to take a mini vacation to get away from the daily routine. But for the last couple years, she wasn't able to go anywhere. She didn't feel like going anywhere. Without Shahil, life meant nothing to her. His absence affected her mentally, emotionally and physically; she didn't want to go out anymore.

As Suri was a very enthusiastic and energetic little girl, she got tired of staying at home. She kept asking Sonya: "Mom, when is Daddy coming back? It looks like he will never come back. Mom, all the girls in my class are planning to take a vacation to different places. Can we take a vacation now?"

Suri was fond of horseback riding, camping and visiting parks. The last time the family went horseback riding was five years ago. It was in the spring too. Sonya and Shahil drove one hundred fifty miles far, somewhere near the Pocono mountains, just to go horseback riding; they also enjoyed the scenic view along the way. Suri remembered that time, so she was forcing Sonya to take her somewhere. Sonya promised her that they would go next year when her Dad was back. Sonya hated to promise things like that as she didn't know when Shahil would return, but she decided to dare a short trip for the kids' happiness by next summer.

One Sunday, Sonya received a visitor, who had two children of Suri's age. In fact, Neil and Vicky were Suri's friends, but due to the cold winter, they had not visited for a long time. Suri got so excited to see them that she asked permission to play behind the tall trees, creating their tree club behind the tree.

For the most part, Sonya trusted the kids, so Sonya and the guests let them play behind the tree. Sonya, her mom and the guest were so busy talking that they didn't realize time passing by.

When the guest was ready to leave, Sonya went outside to call the kids. She didn't see all three kids behind the tree. Sonya called them by names, "Suri, Vicky, Neil where are you?" She had no reply. The guest started to worry too. Sonya and the guests walked to the street checking all the backyards. They, even, called loud by names, so kids could here them, but they couldn't find them. Her friend started to cry thinking what worst could happen. After long time search around her area, they had to call the police. The police came and searched the neighborhood. Meanwhile, Sonya's neighbor told her that she would drive to the creek and near the woods to look for the kids.

In a few minutes, her neighbor came back with all three kids. She found them playing in the woods near the creek; they were chasing the birds. Sonya and her guest were so happy to see them, but then got so angry for going somewhere without telling them. All three kids started to cry and apologized. In fact, while they were playing behind the tree, they started to play some other games and they ran to the woods, stayed there, and started to chase after birds. They completely forgot to tell their parents. The police filled out a report and left. Sonya's neighbor knew that this was the second occasion, and she warned Sonya about losing custody of her kids if it happened again. Sonya thought of her never ending problems being single parent and grounded Suri for a week and demanded that Suri always informed her of her whereabouts.

32. Pool Party

Summer was approaching fast and schools were ending pretty soon. One evening, Suri came home from school with two invitation cards from two of her classmates. One was a birthday party invitation from her best friend, Katie, and another was from her friend Tanya for a pool party in the summer. She was jumping with excitement. She got ready with the swimsuits and birthday gifts.

She attended Katie's birthday party, where she had a great time with the clown, the face painting, singing songs together and playing games with other classmates. She stayed there longer than most other classmates as Katie's Mom liked Suri so much. Suri was invited to play with Katie many times, so Sonya had no problem with it.

Suri also went to Tanya's pool party. She was afraid to swim in the deeper water. Most of her friends were able to swim in deep water, but Suri didn't really know how to swim. Nonetheless, she had a good time eating pizza and ice cream at the pool. Her pleasant time was ruined as she felt ashamed in front of her classmates. When Suri came home, she cried as some of her classmates didn't like Suri; Suri didn't like them as they made fun of Suri for not knowing how to swim really well.

From that moment on, Sonya decided to forget about her life problems and pay more attention to her children's future. She started to inquire about swimming lessons, dance class, girl scouts and girls sports. Sonya was spending most of her evenings, taking the children to their lessons. She even told her mom to keep dinner ready so as soon as she came home from work, she could take the children to their classes.

Krish was five year old and he needed training as much as Suri did. She signed him up for a sport and the boy scouts. Most of the time a father would come to drop the child or stay with them for boy's sport team. Krish wouldn't play well as he was feeling shy. Sonya thought that Krish had forgotten his dad, as it had been a long time since his departure. But, Krish was feeling ashamed, as he had no daddy. Sonya would try to inspire him by saying encouraging words and say, "Daddy is out of the country and he will return once his work project is finished."

As Krish started to go to preschool, he made some friends. He already had some friends in the neighborhood. They would play together outside the house, but they also started to come into the house to play with Krish. Most of the time, his friend's dad would come to pick them up for evening supper. As soon as his friend's dad would arrive, Krish would hide behind the door, and would peek through the door as if he was afraid of him as if he would afraid of big man and missing something. He would come out from behind the door only after they leave. He wouldn't say anything to Sonya as he was more attached to his grandma. He would run to grandma's lap, put his hands around her neck, and whisper in her ear, "Grandma, how come I have no daddy when everyone else has one." Listening to his innocent question, Sonya's mom would cry for a while and would sigh as if her own son's world was lost and stolen. She would give the same answer to Krish as Sonya did to Suri. This would happen every so often. Even when a repairman came to the house, he would hide behind the door. He might have a pain deep inside his heart for missing dad, which he wasn't able to understand.

As Sonya dealt with many different experiences in her life, she became familiar with many things in life. She started to inquire about community occasions being celebrated in the neighborhood parks, schools and many other places. She started to take the kids to Halloween fire camp nights at a nearby park organized by the park commission. She would take them for hayrides; she also enjoyed the country life along with her kids. She would take them hiking in the mountains, a trip organized by some association. She would go to school trips along with Suri and Krish to the Zoo or Apple Orchid or even some musical play or movie. She went on camping trips organized by the girl scouts and the boy scouts, where she enjoyed the nature most. She helped with their school homework and their school projects. As Sonya didn't attend school in this country, she wasn't familiar with the library system. But Sonya asked the librarian for help. Sonya felt as if she had become a school kid again. She tried to give her children all the love she could muster until Shahil's return. She had an unconditional love for her kids.

33. First Ballet

It was almost a year since Suri joined the Belle Dance Class. The training was over for the first year, and now it was time for her first recital in the hall. Suri was going to practice every day. She paid for the dress and got her "Tutu" as her recital dress. She tried it on and looked at herself in the mirror smiling because the dress was so beautiful.

On the day of the recital, Sonya took care of her hairstyle and her make-up. She looked beautiful and charming in her belle dress. Sonya took some pictures in the best posture of the belle and taped the occasion as well. Sonya drove her to the hall and took her with her friends to join in a row. The atmosphere was thrilling due to the beautiful Belle dancers, their dresses and their hairstyles.

The show started and the little dancers appeared one after another according to the class. Now it was the turn of Suri's class. So far, Suri was fine and excited, but as soon as her class was up on stage, she got scared. This was her first time performance on stage in front of an audience, so it was natural for her to get nervous. They hadn't started the performance yet, so Sonya instantly ran to the stage and whispered something into her ear that made her smile.

The colorful lights shone onto the stage and Suri was standing in the center of all the girls with style when the music started. It was a beautiful song for the belle dance and all the girls were performing very well. The slow music and the motion was so beautiful that for a moment one was in amusement. At the end, Suri was in the center again with the beautiful belle style, ending the show. Everyone clapped a lot, as it was one of the best performances of the day. As Suri got off the stage to take her seat in the hall along with the other girls, other parents of the class started to complement her as she performed very well.

At the end of the show, everyone got some kind of prize or medal, but Suri's class was the first as a prizewinner, and Suri got first prize in her class. Sonya was so happy to see her first performance and to be a proud mother. Sonya and other parents gave her flowers as she was getting off the stage. Suri was upset and nervous at first, but now she was a proud performer. She wished Shahil could have seen her first performance. He would have been a proud father too. This was the first good and pleasant experience after a long time.

34. Bee sting

Sonya's mom took Suri out to the woods as her treat for performing well in dance class. Suri loved to go to the woods, and her grandma liked to walk around the street every summer time to get some fresh air and some exercise.

In the evening, Suri and her grandma arrived back home, but her grandma was not feeling well. She had a bee sting on her foot, but she wouldn't tell Sonya anything about her problem. She felt that her daughter had enough responsibility and she didn't want to bother her.

Life wasn't easy for Sonya. The responsibility was overwhelming her. She had fears and anxieties all that time and they kept knocking at her door. She was juggling with her job, paying the bills on time, the housework, raising two kids, and of course, she had to take care of Shahil's case too. She kept working hard as long as in order to keep her family secure and happy.

After a couple hours, Sonya's mom slowly walked to her bedroom. Sonya saw swollen foot, which was dark red by now. Sonya got scared and asked her what had happened. After her mom explained the situation, Sonya thought she must be taken to the emergency room. If she was allergic to the bee sting, she could die of it. So far, she never had to go to the hospital other than for the kids' regular check-up. She truly thanked the Lord for keeping her family members healthy. She thought of the nearest hospital in her area, but she couldn't leave the children home alone as they were too young. She didn't want to bother her friends to come to her house to stay overnight as they were living far away, and they had to go to work the next morning too. She didn't know any babysitter in her neighborhood; she never needed a baby sitter as her mom was taking care of her children. She thought about it impatiently as her mom's condition was getting worse. It was a life and death situation so she had to take her to the hospital.

Instantly, she went to the master bedroom to her temple to pray to the Lord. Before she started to pray, tears began to fall. She prayed to the Lord to guard her children while she was away. At this time of the night, she had no choice other than leaving them home alone. She called Suri and slowly asked.

"Suri, could you please stay home alone"?

"No mom, I will be scared to stay by myself. And what about Krish? Are you taking him with you?"

Impatiently, Sonya replied: "You and Krish need to stay home. Just do what I say."

Now Suri started to cry and said, "No, mom, I am too scared and I want to come with you."

Sonya knew they were legally too young to stay home alone. And what if something happened, she thought. She would be responsible for child negligence. Sonya told Suri, "Ok, I am trying to make Krish sleep. And you are my bold girl. Just do what mom says for today, sweetie. Mommy will be thankful to you."

After some good explanation, Suri agreed to take care of Krish and to stay home. Sonya explained to her, "While she is away, if some one knocks the door, do not open and do not answer the phone".

Suri asked her, "then how would you come, if I won't open the door."

Sonya explained her that she would come thru garage door.

Sonya put Krish in bed. When Sonya was ready to leave, she kissed Krish's head and she hugged and kissed Suri too and whispered everything going to be ok, honey. Don't worry. She waved and left. Suri kept starring at her from the window as mom was taking grand mom to the hospital at night.

Sonya drove to the nearest hospital and entered the emergency room. She helped her mom to get out of the car to go into the main office. The nurse registered her for emergency treatment and brought her a wheelchair.

While they took several tests, Sonya prayed for her children's safety. She didn't know how long it would take. She checked with the doctors and even they were not sure. Yet, they assured her that her mom would be transferred to a private room soon. She had to stay until her condition would improve.

Sonya felt like calling home, but she realized that she had told Suri not to answer the phone. The doctors wouldn't let her go home until mom was taken to the private room. After some more tests, the doctor told her, "Ms. Mehra, it was good that you brought her to the hospital. This is really a serious case. In lots of cases, people die of bee stings." At four o'clock in the morning, Sonya's mom was finally taken to the private room. Sonya was allowed to leave, but she was told to see the doctor at nine o'clock in the morning. Sonya gave them her phone number and told them to call her at home. Sonya quickly left for home.

Sonya drove faster than the speed limit to get home faster. She afraid that she would create another problem by an accident, but it was early in the morning and there wasn't much traffic. As she reached home, she opened her garage door with the remote control and quickly jumped out off the car. She ran upstairs breathlessly, skipping two steps at a time, to check on her kids. As she went to her bedroom, she saw both children sleeping quietly. She went close to them and kissed their heads; they were safe home alone. She looked at the sky from the window. The sky was shining with the stars.

The moon light was shining. She felt like, the angles were watching on her kids sleeping in the bedroom. She thanked the lord for keeping them safe.

For the next two days she took off from work. She would get up early in the morning, prepared the children's breakfast, and got them ready for school. Once they had left, she drove to the hospital to see her mom and come back home when they got back from school. The doctor told her to release her mom within the next two days.

One evening, while grandma was still in the hospital, Krish was playing outside with some other kids, and Sonya was cooking in the kitchen.

Suddenly, Sonya heard a screeching noise from the car................... Chue........eeeeeeeee..... eeeeeeeee............... Sonya ran towards the window to see what had happened. Then Sonya screamed, "Oh my god! Oh my god!" She saw Krish thrown on the sidewalk, and his bike in the air. Obviously, the car had hit Krish's bike and it looked like deadly accident. She ran outside, and held her son in her hand. She started to scream...... help..... some one help.........help.... A few neighbors ran outside and called the ambulance. They told Sonya to go to hospital while they would report to the police. Her neighbor joined her too. Krish was unconscious at the time, but he was breathing according to the nurse in the ambulance.

Krish was immediately taken to the emergency room. Impatiently, Sonya was waiting outside for the doctor. An hour later, the doctor called her in and told her that he had fractured his leg, but he would be fine otherwise. Sonya shook the doctor's hands and thanked him. The doctor allowed Sonya to see Krish. He lay in bed with his eyes barely open. As soon as Krish saw his mom, he said slowly, "Mom, it wasn't my fault." He was afraid that his mother was mad at him for riding his bike down the hill onto the street.

Sonya always stopped him to run his bike from the hill down to the road. As he was growing, he was becoming mischievous and ran his bike carelessly. Fortunately, he had put his helmet on. Sometime he wouldn't listen and run his bike without putting on his helmet.

Sonya said, "Honey, don't worry about whose fault it is, as long as you are ok." She hugged him dearly, and cried for a while. She could have lost him today, and she couldn't bear the thought of it. She thanked the lord for saving him. Krish was an "Apple of eye". What, if, Shahil would know that his apple of the eye is in the hospital! Krish had a cast on his leg and had to stay in the hospital for a week. Sonya decided not to tell Shahil about this.

Sonya's mom was worried as Sonya didn't show up that day at all. When Sonya went to see her, she didn't want to tell her about Krish's accident. Her mom loved Krish so much, even more than her own son. And if she knew about the accident, Sonya didn't know what her reaction could be. Her mom could get a heart attack. Sonya decided not to tell her anything until she was released from the hospital. Sonya told her that she was simply worn out, mentally and physically, from running between the hospital and home.

Two days later, her mom was released from the hospital and learned about the situation. She almost broke down knowing that Krish was in the hospital too. She was praying to the lord, asking him whose evil eye was on this beautiful family that never came out of trouble. She thanked the lord for saving her dear grandson and asked for blessings for this family. But she also got upset with Sonya for not taking proper care of her dear grandson while she was in the hospital. Most grandmas would pride themselves of how good they were taking care of their grandchildren. Sonya's mom wasn't an exception.

Suri was staying with the family's best friends Milan and Nikki. Sonya called them as she had no choice left. Milan and Nikki along with Suri came to see Sonya's mom and her son Krish. They were very mad at Sonya, as she didn't call them more often for help. Sonya told them that she was thankful to them anyways, as they were helping her even without calling them. Sonya was determined not to trouble anybody more than necessary.

With Krish being at home, Sonya's responsibility doubled as she had to give him a bath, help him dress and walk around the house on crutches. Sonya hoped that Krish at least learned a lesson from this accident.

35. Jessica and wall paper

A couple weeks later, Sonya went back to work. Her boss was concerned about her absences for so long. Her in-bin in her office was piled up with files that needed to be approved. Some of them needed urgent attention. Mike tried to take care of some work in his busy work schedule, but he didn't have enough time. Sonya started to work quickly on the files.

Her best friend Jessica stopped by and knocked a couple times. Sonya didn't hear her, as she was pretty busy working. Jessica came in and came close to her ears and said, "Hallo, Sonya, it's me." Sonya looked up, and said, "Oh! You scared me." She was happy to see Jessica after long time. She offered Jessica a seat in a chair opposite her desk. Sonya took some time off to talk to her since they hadn't seen each other for a while. After some chitchat, Jessica went back to her office. As Jessica had been promoted to a higher position and had moved to a different building, Sonya hardly got to see her. Sonya enjoyed seeing her in the mornings. She slipped in the past for a moment.

Jessica was a young and energetic girl, who started her career as an IT manager in the same department a couple years ago. Every time Jessica passed by her office, she would say "hi" trying to start to talk to her. But as Sonya was shy, she wouldn't talk to her. As time passed by, they slowly got to know each other. Each morning, Jessica would pass by Sonya's office with her coffee mug. Her coffee would smell so good that once Sonya stopped her to talk about her coffee. After that, Jessica started to stop by her office almost all morning. As she was a very important and busy person, she would stop by only for a few minutes.

She was highly professional and an individual with dignity. Sonya noticed that there were so many professionals in the world, but few of them had dignity. Dignity related to morals, ethics, and a better lifestyle. As more and more people were accepting the modern way of junky lifestyle and trash talk, it had become a permissible behavior for children and teens, which greatly affected the business conduct too. Jessica was different in this manner and Sonya loved the way she talked to her about different subjects. She would talk in such a sweet and slow voice, that Sonya loved to listen to her. She seemed to be intelligent and Sonya always loved intellectual people, as debating was her favorite subject. Those few minutes in the morning would give Sonya a day full of tonic.

Sonya and Jessica became best friends and started to go out for lunch and even to the movies. Sometimes, they would just walk through the city and go to famous stores. Jessica would buy costly gift items, but Sonya wouldn't buy anything due to her financial responsibility. As soon as Shahil arrived back home, she would be able to do anything she wanted to.

Sonya always loved the high quality lifestyles. She had envisioned America as the country of high lifestyles. As more immigrants started to come to this country, its quality of life had been lowered, as most people preferred to buy cheaper items. As Sonya became familiar with most of the good stores in Center City, she decided to buy gifts for her family members back home sometime, as she wasn't able to visit them now.

Once, Sonya was in a meeting and Jessica stopped by her office. She saw a poem hanging on the wall. She stopped to read that poem. It was about life and it was a summary of a famous religious scripture. It read:

What is Life?

Life is a Challenge	Meet it
Life is a Gift	Accept it
Life is an Adventure	Dare it
Life is a Sorrow	Overcome it
Life is a Tragedy	Face it
Life is a Duty	Perform it
Life is a Game	Play it
Life is a Mystery	Unfold it
Life is a Song	Sing it
Life is an Opportunity	Take it
Life is a Journey	Complete it
Life is a Promise	Fulfill it
Life is a Love	Enjoy it
Life is a Beauty	Praise it
Life is a Spirit	Realize it
Life is a Struggle	Fight it
Life is a Puzzle	Solve it
Life is a Goal	Achieve it

As Jessica was reading it, she instantly fell in love with it. When Sonya came back to her office, Jessica asked her if she could have a copy. She was getting her Master's degree, and she had to present an English paper on some subject. She decided to prepare her presentation on life. She did very well on it, and she thanked Sonya for letting her have a copy. She hung that poem in her office too as it had a meaningful message.

Years later, Jessica was promoted and moved to a different building. Sonya missed her a lot on an everyday basis. But once in a while, she would come to see her or they would arrange to go out to lunch.

As Jessica went back to her office, Sonya remembered that poem. It was still hanging on her office wall. In those few years, she hardly noticed it. She went to the wall and started to read it again. She started to think about it seriously as her life had been hectic for so long.

Sonya was thinking of her own problems, as she had to face them without her husband, Shahil. She had a challenge in front of her, which she had to meet. She had a struggle to fight, and she had a goal to achieve. And most of all, she had a spirit, but she had to realize it. She read that poem again and again, and was determined to face the situation happily until Shahil came home.

Sonya used to read religious books during her travel time on the train. Some what, the summary of that book had the same idea as this poem. If the poem about life was true, life was certainly not a problem. A human makes life more critical by not understanding it or by not following it in the right manner. As a human being, one have to learn to calm down and to take time to think over the situation. If they took time to think, it would be easy to solve problems. According to the "Karma" theory, it would be easy to resolve the problems most of the time rather than loosing control of your life from your hand.

Sonya noticed that she had experienced so many changes in her nature too. She used to be aggressive with decision making, but now she had learned to be patient and thoughtful. Sonya learned to control herself by fasting too. Every so often she would choose to fast to stay in balance. The more food she ate, the more imbalanced she was. She read that the less but healthy food you have, the more in control you are. In modern times, "Yoga" had become a famous faster in the western world; it also meant "self control." It might have to do with the self and life. It was a mystery to unfold.

36. Water and the voice

Shahil bought a brand new house a few years ago. He loved a beautiful, well furnished, and well organized house. All the bedrooms had matching carpets with wall colors. He had decorated his house with old-fashioned furniture and antique showpieces. They had famous painter's paintings hanging on the wall. The landscaping was beautifully done. He would keep working around the house in his free time in order to maintain the house. To keep everything perfect, he would repair many things in the house by himself. Through experience, he became a handyman.

Ever since he left, Sonya had many problems in the house. Sonya tried to repair small things by using nails and the hammer, but she couldn't do much with otherwise due to her inexperience. So many things were falling apart, but Sonya couldn't finish it professionally. The water was leaking from the roof and she needed to replace the roof. The panels of the windows had to be replaced. The walls were covered by crayon colors even though she kept cleaning them. Despite of it all, Sonya tried to keep her house neat and clean; nobody would notice the many problems around the house.

The most recent problem occurred with the toilet tank in the bathroom. The water wouldn't stop flushing. Sonya had to take a day off from work. Her vacation time was being used fast. She had an appointment with the plumber who was coming to her house to check on it. The plumber arrived on time and replaced the necessary part in the toilet tank. Sonya gave him a check and got his contact number in case something else went wrong.

On the same weekend, while she was working around the house, she noticed that water was flowing out of the tank to the bathroom floor. She ran to the bathroom to check what was wrong, but the water had already reached out to the bedroom carpet. Sonya panicked and ran to call the plumber. But by the time plumber could come, however, the room would be a mess. She ran around confused and saying oh…my…god…oh…my…god…, not realizing that she could have shut off the water valve.

All of a sudden, she heard a voice: "Wait, don't run."

She was impatient, but she looked back to follow the voice….

She was curious to see where the voice came from. "Just do what I say" said the voice.

She followed the voice.

"Open the lid," said the voice.

As if in trust, Sonya opened the lid.

"You see the red button; press it downwards." said the voice.

Sonya did it and the water instantly stopped flowing. Sonya was breathless due to the disaster, but she instantly ran to the corner of her master bedroom where she kept her little temple.

She said, "Lord, is that you? I know it must be you. Who else can help me at this time? Thanks so much for saving me from big trouble. I don't know what I would have done, if the water had spread to the master bedroom by the time plumber would come. And I didn't have any idea to shut off the valve."

Sonya knelt on the floor to pray to her Lord, still crying and thanking him. She never saw or experienced such a miracle, but that was the real fact for her. She thought, "It's a miracle..... It's a miracle......" She had heard many stories of miracles, but she never believed them. Many people even questioned God's existence. Sonya thought, "Maybe there is God or may be there isn't, but somebody is watching over you as you can call them angels. Some people believe God is nothing but faith."

Many times she felt that an angel was protecting her. Many times she had been saved unknowingly. She thought of the creepy noise at nighttime, the midnight phone calls, walking alone at nighttime, Krish's bike accident, missing children, just to name a few. But this was a completely different experience, as it needed verbal instruction.

She thought her morning prayers were fruitful. She thanked the lord again and again.

Repairmen make mistakes too once in a while. The plumber might have forgotten to set something properly. She thought, it wasn't really a big problem when she followed the voice. The problem was solved instantly with little effort. But, once in a while, little mistake could cause big problem as she could end up living in wet carpet for some few days until insurance company would look at it. She thanked the lord again for saving her from big mess.

37. Ellis Island

Several years passed by fighting for justice and working hard for her family. Sonya couldn't take any vacation time off, as she didn't like to drive long distance and she wasn't familiar with the many different routes and roads. Additionally, she couldn't enjoy her vacation time without Shahil. She had promised Suri to take her on vacation next year. As summer arrived, Sonya thought about what to do and where to go. Sonya felt guilty to entertain herself, while Shahil was in the "Big House". Sonya thought, how long she would upset her children.

How long she would keep them away from their happy time.

As Suri was growing, she was getting smarter. Suri wanted everything her friends had. A good vacation, a birthday celebration, a Christmas celebration — anything she could have. She loved to go to museums in different cities, as history was her favorite subject. She had many dreams to see Egypt, Rome and Paris, and many other ancient countries where history lives. She was a very talkative and charming girl. When she talked about different things, Sonya could see sparkling dreams in her eyes. Although, Sonya wasn't able to go far, she decided to take her to the "Statue of Liberty" and Washington D.C, where she would enjoy seeing a few museums too. Driving into New York would be very difficult for her. She hadn't decided yet as what to do.

During one of her lunch breaks, she saw a "Star Tour" bus waiting outside her office building. As Philadelphia was a historic place, she saw many tour buses coming into the city from different states. She thought it would be a good idea to take the tour bus instead of driving with the kids and taking risks. She saw a toll free phone number on the back of the bus, and she instantly wrote it down on paper. Sonya called that number and asked for the details. Within a few days, she got all the information in the mail. She made a reservation for a visit to the "Statue of Liberty" on Ellis Island. When Suri and Krish knew about the trip, they became really excited. A week later, Sonya packed up for their short trip to Ellis Island.

Sonya, her mom and the two kids went to the pick- up location. Krish took the seat near the window and sat with his grandma. Suri took the seat near the window with Sonya. Sonya noticed that the whole bus was full of senior citizens, who weren't able to drive. There were no kids in the whole bus. She felt ashamed, but this was her first experience and she had paid for the tour, so she had to be there now.

While relaxing, Sonya played games with Krish and Suri. If Krish won a game, he would laugh so hard that other passengers noticed it. His laughter was so sweet. Sonya loved it so much and kissed him every often. It happened several times that some passengers said, "Oh, look at the little boy, he is so sweet. It's so nice to hear him giggling". At a rest stop, some passengers called him over and they hugged and kissed him too. Some passengers gave him candy bars and some passengers, who didn't have anything, they give him cash as a gift. Krish took it happily as he was little and wasn't allowed to carry cash with him. One couple said, "We had an enjoyable ride, we hardly hear any giggling as our children are adults and have moved out of the house." Sonya felt ashamed at first, but now she was happy to see other passengers loving Krish and Suri and giving them hugs and kisses. Krish and Suri were very happy too.

The tour bus finally arrived at the New Jersey port, where everyone had to get off to take the ferry to the Statue of Liberty. The bus driver gave instructions on how to come back and at what time, but Sonya didn't pay much attention as she was out on trip after some few years. She was excited along with the kids and kids were pulling her hands to get out of bus fast. Sonya stayed in line along with other people, until they finally got on the ferry. Within a few minutes, the ferry arrived at Ellis Island.

Sonya got off on Ellis Island and started to walk towards the Statue of Liberty. She got some information from the tourist info center and started to walk around to enjoy the surrounded area before she could go to the top of the Statue. She took some pictures of everybody. Krish and Suri were so happy that they would say "Chee....z... z....z" whenever a photo was taken. She also took some pictures of the Twin Towers in the distance.

Sonya asked Suri and Krish if they wanted to walk to the head of the Statue or if they wanted to take the elevator. Her mom went to a separate waiting line to take the elevator, as she wasn't able to walk too far to the top of the head. Sonya and the children decided to go to the very top. The line was moving so slowly, but Sonya didn't realize it as she was having fun with the kids. Finally, they reached to the top of the Statue of Liberty. Everybody looked outside the window. The statue was surrounded with the water and land. New York City with its high rise buildings looked so beautiful. The Statue was so huge and tall that it amazed Sonya. She wondered how it was built and what a great effort it was to build such a huge statue out of metal. Hours later, they descended again. Everybody was tired of walking and hungry, so they had lunch and rested for a while.

Sonya had time until six o'clock, so she was just waking around. Sonya heard several people screaming, "Oh, my God....It's so bad....." Some people started to cry like their own family member had passed away. Sonya wondered, "What's going on? What's so bad?" Some people had their radio on loud, so others could hear the news as well. One of the famous president's sons was killed in a plane crash. Sonya immediately felt sorry and started to cry, as he was her favorite too.

The news were going on and on continuously and repeatedly. Suddenly, Sonya thought of her friend Jessica, and she started to laugh. Some people looked at her in a cross way as they saw her laugh. Sonya instantly became serious as America was crying and she was laughing. It was weird, but she remembered something that Jessica told her a long time ago.

Jessica had told her about one of her own experiences at a conference in San Diego. Jessica and her husband Steve both had to go to the same conference; many well- known people attended as well. On the first day of the conference, she saw the president's son at another table. He was as handsome as a prince that she was amazed to see him and couldn't wait to meet him. She saw his pictures in many magazines. She used to love his handsome personality that she used to call him her second husband. That day she saw him personally and thought he was really a handsome guy. She got up from her table and whispered to her husband that she was going to see her second husband. Her husband's laughter drew attention from the other attendees. He said, "Go…go…, and see your second husband." Jessica went to his table, and introduced herself. They shook hands, and after some talk she went back to her own table.

When Jessica told this story to Sonya, she looked happy to have met the son of the president. That memory brought on Sonya's laughter at the Statue of Liberty. Sonya imagined Jessica would be very upset about the news. How lucky are those famous people that people from around the world love them! And today the world was crying upon hearing the sad news.

It was almost 5:30 p.m. Sonya didn't realize how fast time had passed by. Sonya immediately left to take the first ferry. Sonya got on the ferry without any questions. When the ferry stopped, Sonya and kids got off and walked to their stop. She felt everything looked different in the evening; she couldn't find their bus stop. She went to different bus stop, where other tour bus stopped, but she couldn't find her bus. It was almost dark and she started to worry, as they had no means to go home.

Finally, Sonya contacted the police and explained her situation. The police told her that she must have taken the wrong ferry as this was the New York port. Sonya realized that the bus driver had announced something important, but Sonya and her kids had been so excited that she didn't care to listen. Now she realized the difference of New York port as it was crowded and New Jersey Port as it was quite and greener. She was confused now, and didn't know how to get home. She asked the police about what she could do now. The police suggested to her to take a train to Philadelphia. Sonya called a taxi to go to the train station. She found out that the train to Philadelphia had just left and the next train wouldn't leave for another three hours. Her mom and kids were so tired of walking so Sonya got very upset and started to cry. The only choice they had left was to take a taxi home. Even though it cost thrice as much, Sonya picked one of the nicest cabdrivers, so they could go home safely. Finally, late at night, they came home frustrated and tired. Looking at up in the sky….she murmered, Oh God!why it had to be in my first trip!

38. New evidence

Sonya went to work as usual but she couldn't forgive herself for making such a mistake for not paying attention on bus driver's instruction. As it happened, all humans made mistakes. And just like any other person in the world, she needed some entertainment and rest as well. If Shahil were here, she would simply have gone to work, come home, cook, clean, and rest. She hoped for that time to come soon.

Sonya wanted to give the kids a good treat so they would not remember the bad time. Sonya wanted to do something, but for last several days, she felt that something was going to happen soon. Her left eye was twitching several times a day. Her never-ending problems kept emerging one after another. But Suri and Krish were like her two eyes. Like two beautiful roses in her garden, she received energy from them, looking forward towards their future. Suri was sweet as a doll and Krish's laughter was so sweet that she only had to hear it once to forget all of her problems.

Sonya was busier than usual at work. She didn't have enough time to check her voice messages or check her e-mails. She had audits going on in her office for the past two weeks. She was responsible to answer questions by the State auditors and to provide the required paperwork. She provided them with everything they needed in a matter of minutes, so the auditors were pleased with her expediency. While auditors had lunch, Sonya checked her e-mails and voice messages. There was one message from her lawyer to come and see him as soon as possible.

Sonya panicked. She had been waiting for the new evidence for a long time. Did Mr. James Brown get the new evidence? Why did he want to see her as soon as possible? This was Shahil's last chance, so she was very upset. She decided to go home instead of going to the lawyer's office. She went home and told her mom not to disturb her as she wasn't feeling well. All she wanted to do was sleep. She was utterly depressed.

She woke up early the next day, got ready, took her breakfast and went to work. She felt more refreshed. On the train, instead of reading something, she just sat near the window and kept looking outside. She wanted to see the lawyer today, but she was hesitant. What would he tell her? She thought hard about her past life. She had no energy to take more bad news. Finally, she told herself, "Sonya, just go and see him. Take it easy. Whatever it may be, just relax and take it easy."

At lunchtime, she went to the lawyer's office. The lawyer had a client in his office, so Sonya waited outside. She was very impatient and so upset that she went to the rest room at least three to four times. The secretary saw her very upset, but she didn't know much about her case, so she couldn't tell her anything other than "relax, Everything will be ok..." After waiting for a long time, Mr. Brown called her in. Sonya went in impatiently.

"Hello, Ms. Sonya. How are you?" He wanted to shake her hand, but Sonya had no energy to get up and shake his hand.

Sonya simply said: "I am fine."

Mr. Brown said, "You don't look fine to me, but guess what?

I have very good news for you though." Sonya's nervous face brightened and her eyes widened out of curiosity.

Mr. Brown said, "I got the engineer's report, saying that Shahil's car's tire doesn't match the print. The tracks they have can't possibly be from your car. I have details of that report."

Sonya was speechless, looking at him with teary eyes with surprise. She leaned back and said, "Oh! Finally, I have good news. I just can't believe it…I just can't believe it…." She repeated it a couple times. "It's been so long time for me to have any kind of good news. I just can't believe it… I just can't believe it." She repeated again with tears running on her cheeks. Mr. Brown also became a little emotional. Then Sonya said, "Now tell me, what you are going to do." "Well, as I told you before, I have to take this new evidence to the court and submit an appeal, which may take another six to eight months."

After some discussion, Sonya got up to leave his office. Mr. Brown came to leave her out of the office. Sonya shook his hand and gave a hug to the secretary as she was happy to have a good news after so much struggle.

39. 7ᵗʰ Birthday

Sonya wanted to celebrate the kids' birthdays in a special manner. She hadn't been celebrating any birthdays so far because she was feeling guilty to have any entertainment in the house without Shahil. But now she wanted to make Suri and Krish very happy by inviting their classmates. She prepared a list of things to do.

Suri and Krish were born in the same summer month. Sonya decided to celebrate Krish's birthday first and Suri's second. She decided to call Krish's favorite TV show character and clown for his celebration. She went shopping for party decorations and other supplies.

She prepared bags for his classmates and filled them up with items children like best. She got the best invitation cards If you opened it, it would sing "Happy Birthday." Sonya also thought about making a special cake.

Sonya and Suri discussed the cake decoration. Sonya had some suggestions, but Suri kept saying no to everything. Krish used to play with roaring dinosaur toys and watched dinosaur movie cassettes as he loved their roaring noise and huge animals. He had class project to create a dinosaur jungle, too. He loved to finish that project. Suri suggested decorating the cake with small pieces of dinosaur toys and other jungle items. Sonya liked the idea.

The night before the celebration, Sonya bought a big sheet of cake. Suri and Sonya both decorated it with small toys. In half an hour, she created a beautiful jungle with toy trees, grass, dinosaurs and dinosaur eggs. It looked so beautiful; Krish would love it. She decorated the house with banners and lots of colorful balloons and other party supplies. She had a music candle, but she chose plain candles instead, as she wanted to hear kids singing loud "Happy Birthday."

On the day of the birthday celebration, the classmates arrived one after another. Their parents also came in to say Happy Birthday to Krish and complimented the decoration, and particularly the cake decoration. Krish's favorite TV character and the clown also arrived on time. As soon as they came in, they started to play their own music.

Kids started to dance along with the music and the TV character "Arthur". They had music for the chicken dance and the Hockey Pokey, both of which the kids loved very much. After the dance, the clown put on a magic show, and it was very enjoyable to hear the "wow" from all the kids. After the magic show, they had face painting and balloon toys. As they had enjoyable time, Sonya heard laughter and giggling voice in the room. Sonya felt like she was in a different world.

Now was the time to cut the cake. Sonya quickly put the cake on the table, and put the candles on it and lighted the candle. Everybody started to sing: "Happy Birthday to you! Happy Birthday to you, dear Krish! How old are you, how old are you?" Krish closed his eyes, wished for his Daddy to come home and blew out the seven candles.

Everybody took a piece of cake; pizza and soda were served. Krish was curious to open his gifts, so Sonya put all the gifts in the middle of the room. The kids sat in a circle around Krish. Krish opened his gifts one after another. As he was opening them, he kept saying, "Wow,

I love this." He got some gift certificates to toy stores, and he got some money. He loved everything.

There was some free time until the parents arrived to pick up their children. Sonya took them out in the yard to play some games. They played on the swing and the slide sets as well as other games. At the end of the day, kids left and Krish was very happy with his "only Special" day.

It was mid-summer when Sonya prepared for Suri's birthday. Suri invited all her classmates and a few other girls from the neighborhood as well. She wanted to have a sleep-over party. Sonya bought some art and craft supplies so the girls could have an enjoyable time. Sonya prepared for the party just as she did for Krish's.

All the girls arrived with their sleeping bags. They celebrated Suri's birthday and played until late into the night. Sonya could hear lots of laughing and giggling from the girls, which made her very happy. She wished Shahil could hear it too.

40. Guest & Tour

Sonya went to work. Most employees were on vacation. When co-workers came, they described their experiences. She was dying to have some vacation time, but without Shahil her vacation wouldn't be a vacation. Shahil was interested in natural places. He loved beaches and lakes, hiking in the mountains and camping. Sonya and the kids would love that too. She would also love to see her family back home, as she hardly had any family here. She used to have a good time with all the family members getting together at one place for almost all occasions. They would talk late into the night, tell jokes and even sing songs together.

She used to get letters and phone calls from family members all this time. They would cry over the phone to see Sonya and her two kids. She missed them a lot. Her biggest inspiration was one of her cousins, her best friend from childhood. She was a poet and she would write poetic and philosophical letters that Sonya kept reading four to five times. Even after that she would carry them in her office bag to read them during lunch. Sonya wished that she could write letters like that as well.

Her cousin's letters eased her pain in her loneliness. This time she received good news from her cousin. She wrote that her parents were coming to visit her brother, who was Sonya's cousin too, living in New York. Sonya was excited to see them. She would be seeing her uncle and aunt again.

A few weeks later, Sonya got a phone call from her cousin in New York. She talked to him and his parents. Sonya invited them to stay with her family. They agreed to stay for one week, and they were going to bring their friends, a couple from Sonya's town. Sonya was very happy to hear the news and looked forward to their arrival. She would be able to answer Suri's usual question, "How come I have no uncles and aunts here?" Sonya explained to her that she had many uncles and aunts back home. She would see them all when they would go to India for a visit.

Sonya had some plans for her guests. After all, they were coming from overseas; they would enjoy going to seev some wonderful places. Working in center city for some few years, Sonya knew that there were many important places to see. After all, Philadelphia is a historic place, and used to be the capital of the United States too. There were many museums, historic buildings and malls all around the city. She decided to gather some information before they arrived at her house.

The next day, Sonya visited the tourist information center located right in the heart of Philadelphia. She started to look at the rack filled with information flyers. She selected some and asked some questions to the person in charge. She got some more information on how to use buses and trains, as it was very hard to drive and park in the city.

41. Phila visit

It was a nice evening in the summer. Sonya was helping her mom with the cooking and dinner preparation. She laid the table with their best china. The hand carved beautiful dinning table looked more beautiful with dinner plates on it. Sonya was waiting for her uncles and aunts as the time was almost 6:00 p.m. When the door bell rang, Sonya ran to the door to receive the guests.

As she opened the door, her cousin, his wife, and the aunts and uncles entered. She welcomed and hugged them all. Sonya's mom was very happy to see her own cousins. They chatted for a while and got ready for dinner. Everybody laughed and joked while they had dinner together. The kids were having fun with their uncles and aunts. Krish took his dinner while sitting on one of his uncles' lap. After dinner, they talked and talked until late into the night. Sonya expressed her wish to take them out and told them her plans for the week.

As planned, Sonya discussed the places they were about to see. Philadelphia, the "city of brotherly love" had many attractions such as historic sites, parks, museums and archives, and performing arts throughout the region – just to name a few.

William Penn, the founder, envisioned Philadelphia as a "green country" anchored by squares of lush, grassy land. Over time, it grew into a large, bustling city with skyscrapers and an abundance of concrete sidewalks. But unlike other large metropolitan areas, Philadelphia continued to have a wealth of parks and greenery, making outdoor enjoyment a reality.

On the first day, Sonya took them out on a tour of the historic sites such as City Hall, the Liberty Bell, the Masonic Temple and Independence Mall. Around mid- afternoon, Suri and Krish grew tired of walking. They decided to take a break, buy some food and rest. While the elders were chatting, Suri and Krish slept on their uncle and aunt's lap. Half an hour later, they visited the Liberty Bell and Independence Hall, two of the most treasured monuments celebrating American freedom.

It was late evening and everyone wanted to go home, but the kids wanted to go on a horse carriage ride. Sonya hired a horse buggy, which took them around the city for half an hour. They went home tired but very happy with their experience of American history. It was a unique, amazing and unexpected experience.

On the second day, Sonya decided to take them out to see museums and other family fun places. They visited "Love Park," and the Museum of Art, just before sunset to catch a spectacular view of Center City. Flickering lights from downtown skyscrapers and cars driving along the famous parkway set a romantic mood as the sun went down.

Finally, they had a fine dinner in one of the famous restaurants. The guests expressed their gratitude to Sonya for taking them out for three days. It was a memorable time for them. Sonya lived in the city, but she hadn't even seen any of those places. The kids were very happy going out with their uncles and aunts. For the remainder of the time, they decided to stay home and have fun with the family.

For the past month, Suri had been practicing for the Belle dance. This time she entered for the state competition, and it took place in one of the best halls of the city. Sonya invited her family guests to see the dance show and bought a few more tickets for them.

On the day before the competition, Suri went to her room to get ready. Suri came running out of her room, and went straight to the garage. She was too shy to show herself to the guests in her ballet dress. Sonya took her to the practice room as it was fun to see all the cute little girls practicing. Finally, practice was over and last suggestions were given to all the girls to do their best in the state level performance. They hoped to get the prize; they had for the past two years.

Saturday morning was beautiful. Suri got up early in the morning, as she was excited to go to the performance. She was also happy that after the show, she would be free for months and she wouldn't have to practice for a while. Sonya finished her morning chores and prepared lunch for the guests. After some free time, everybody got ready to go to the show. As always, Sonya took care of Suri's hair and make-up.

She looked so beautiful that everybody kept staring. They complimented her on her good looks.

Sonya drove to the Center for the Performing Arts, a world class art facility situated in center city.

The city skyline was lit with sparkling lights at night and its streets were bustling. Music echoed throughout the city every day of the week. Whatever your taste, there was a special beat for everyone from 1940' rhythms and sound to the 70's, to the latest jazz fusion, rock, hip-hop and gospel music.

Sonya entered in the hall and took a seat in the VIP section as a parent and guest of the performer. Within a few minutes, the performance began. The theater atmosphere was thrilling. The colorful lights were moving with the performers. Sonya had always preferred ballet to jazz and tap dance. Ballet was well known for its unique features and techniques such as Pointe work and high extensions as well as its graceful, precise movements and ethereal qualities. The movement gave the illusion that the dancer was floating. Ballet was one of the most well preserved dances in the world. Sonya wanted Suri to learn ballet for this reason.

It was the time for Suri's class performance. As their names were declared, Sonya got excited.

A chill passed through her body. She noticed Suri in the center. It was a beautiful song and the girls were very conscious about their body motion. They performed it very well. As it finished, Sonya heard claps for a long time from the audience. It was clear that everybody liked the song and the dance. A few more dances had to be performed before the results were declared. Of course, Sonya and the guests were very curious.

Suri's class received the first prize for the third time in a row. Suri got a medal as best performer of the class. Sonya had tears in her eyes when she saw Suri getting her award medal. She wished Shahil were here to see his dear daughter getting the first prize medal. When Suri came down to see her, Sonya and the family guests hugged her; she received many compliments on her performance. Some people from the audience got up and gave her flowers too. Sonya went home with many happy memories of that day.

Sonya's uncle and aunt had spent a nice time with the family. They felt sorry about what was going on in Sonya's life. Uncle Sam couldn't wait to ask her about Shahil.

Uncle Sam: told her, "Sonya, I know that you don't like to discuss anything, but if you don't mind let me know what's happening." Sonya told him about the new evidence and the new appeal her lawyer had submitted to the court. They read the copy of the appeal. In fact, both uncles were lawyers in different fields. They wished her best of luck for the upcoming result. They chatted until late into the night, as it was the last night of their stay. They even played games with Suri and Krish. The kids were very happy to have met their uncles and aunts.

On Sunday afternoon, Sonya's cousin came to her house to pick them up. It was such a pleasant week that Sonya felt very sorry to say goodbye to them. Sonya's mom cried, as the time to leave was close. They hugged each other; they kissed the kids and took their seat in the car. They waved their hands as car started to run. Sonya kept staring after the running car for a few minutes.

42. Kids home alone and accident

Back at work, the files had piled up on her desk again. She worked until late evenings to catch up with the work. Once she accomplished the task, she called James Brown to inquire about the appeal. Her hands were shaking, as it was their last hope to win the case. She called but hung up the phone before it even started to ring. She was too afraid to talk to her lawyer. She thought what if lawyer had to say something negative? What if, her final hope would be crushed! Sometime she felt to suicide with her problematic situation, but she had Suri and Krish, the apples of her eyes in front of her and she would stop thinking about that.

Then a thought passed through her mind, "What if Shahil wins?" Even though it was just for a moment, many dreams started to emerge. As soon as she realized that she was dreaming, she blinked her eyes and stopped herself. So far, all her attempts were in vain. Every appeal for the parole was declined as Shahil wouldn't give a written statement of his involvement. Shahil strictly told them that he would rather die than admit responsibility for something he didn't commit.

Finally, she dared to call her lawyer and talked to him. He informed her that the results would arrive in a few weeks. He told her that as soon as he knew about the result, he would call her first. Sonya took a deep breath, as she didn't have the energy to hear bad news. This time she hoped for good news.

After a long day of hard work, Sonya went home tired. Her mom looked upset, but didn't say anything as she didn't want to upset Sonya. She had been with Sonya for long time, taking care of her two kids. Now she wanted to see her grown children back home. But how would she travel there? What would happen to

Krish and Suri? She loved them so much. She hated the thought of putting them into daycare or leaving them with a babysitter.

Every night, Sonya would visit to her mom's room to make sure everything was fine. When Sonya entered to her mom's room, Sonya saw her mom sat on the bed. Sonya asked if something was wrong. Her mother explained that she was short of breath. She instantly decided to take her to the emergency room.

She woke up Suri to tell them that she had to go to the hospital. Sonya didn't want to leave them home alone again, but it was too late at night to call a friend. Suri was very upset and didn't want to stay home alone, especially since she remembered the midnight phone calls. But as Sonya explained grandma's situation, Suri agreed teary- eyed to stay home. By this time, Suri had become smart to understand mom's situation. She knew not to open the door or answer the phone. Quickly, Sonya realized that she might need to call her, so she told her to pick up only when the phone rang three times, stopped, and then rang again. Suri agreed and hugged her mom. Sonya got emotional with twice occurred situation, hugged her and told her to take care of Krish.

At the emergency room, Sonya's mom had a lot of trouble breathing, so she was taken very quickly. After some tests, her mom was transferred to a private room and Sonya was able to leave early in the morning.

She rushed out of the hospital, and drove faster than usual. She was concerned about Suri and Krish. Absent- mindedly, she forgot to stop at a stop sign. At this point, she was only a couple miles away from home. She had to pay attention now to make sure she wouldn't get into an accident. She thought, after all traffic laws are for our safety, why to disobey laws.

She was almost close to her house, just couple miles away. Just then she heard a noise and felt some impact. While she was making a left turn, she looked right and left and again right but another fast coming car hit her side. The hood was almost badly bent, but she was not hurt.

She got out of the car to check on the other driver; he was unconscious. Immediately, she shouted for help, ... help.....someone help......... but there was nobody on the road that early in the morning. The roads were very quiet and dark. She opened the door and shook the person, "Hello, sir, are you ok? Are you ok?" Slowly, the injured person opened his eyes. The car's front was totaled; he wasn't even able to drive to home. He had a big bump on his head, and blood was running down his face.

He called the police to report the accident. The police came and took all the information from both parties to report accident. Sonya's car was in bad shape, but she was still able to drive home. She decided to run her car anyway she could as Suri and Krish were home alone.

At home, she ran upstairs breathlessly to see Suri and Krish. Fortunately, they were both sleeping quietly. The sky was shinning bright with the full moon light. The moon light was coming thru the window of her master bed room, throwing it's beautiful white shining cool rays on Suri and Krish's face on the bed. For few moments Sonya kept starring at their innocent faces, the faces of two angels who had nothing to worry about. Sonya looked at the bright moon, thanked the Lord for keeping their angel around, and slipped into bed between Suri and Krish.

43. Shahil won

Sonya wanted to take a couple days off from work to rest. She asked her boss, who replied jokingly, "Oh, what will I do without you; we have so much to do."

Sonya laughed and said, "You will be fine, have fun with some more to do". In the end, Mike approved her vacation time.

Sonya slept until late morning that day. She felt so fresh that she finished all her payments and took care of other matters as well. She took her family to the mall that evening to take care of her shopping. Her kids enjoyed that evening with Sonya. Sonya was passing the time waiting for the result. She just couldn't tell anyone, but her mind wouldn't set anywhere. As she came home, she heard a voice message from her lawyer to see him as soon as possible.

Sonya was twisting and turning from side to side in her bed. She couldn't sleep that night. She thought, why her lawyer wouldn't leave actual massage at the same time? May be it's something.....She couldn't think much about it. If Shahil wasn't freed this time what would happen to her life? Tears were running down from her face. Tired of thinking, she finally fell asleep early in the morning.

The next morning, she went to her little temple and prayed to the Lord to set her free from all the trouble. She stayed there for little longer than usual kneeling down and praying for help. She prayed to lord, "Lord, this time you must be kind or I wouldn't be able to live. Have some mercy on me, Lord." She couldn't stop crying. Finally, she went to get ready to go to lawyer's office. It was cold afternoon. She put on her fur coat, a scarf and a pair of gloves and left.

Sonya was in the train, thinking what her lawyer would talk about. Had the decision been made or did he want to talk about something else? He might have some question.... who knows.....! Usually, she would read some magazine or book to pass the time. But, she couldn't touch anything today. The traveling time seemed too long, as she was impatient to see the lawyer.

At the lawyer's office, she had to wait again for a long period of time. Sonya was growing impatient, and she felt to scream at the lawyer but she just couldn't do that. Finally, she was called into his office.

Mr. Brown greeted her, and then said: "Ms. Mehra, I know you have been waiting for the result for a long time."

Sonya's eyes became wider as she was listening to him. Mr. Brown could see her being impatient. Before Mr. Brown said something, tears running down to her cheek.

Mr. Brown: Are you ok, Ms. Sonya Mehra? I haven't said anything yet. I hope, your family is fine.

Mr. Brown was taking easy while he was talking to Sonya. But Sonya's pain grew deeper as she became more impatient. She felt like she will faint soon. Mr. Brown handed her a tissue out of the tissue box.

Mr. Brown: Relax, Ms. Sonya....you must take care of yourself.

Sonya wiped her teary eyes and tried to put herself together to listen whatever Mr. Brown had to say.....good or bad.....news...... She closed her eyes for a minute.

Mr. Brown: "Guess what Ms. Mehra"!

Sonya looked at him not sure what she will hear.

It will be all over now. Shahil won the case based on the new evidence."

Sonya kept looking at him in disbelief with her mouth a gaped, with more tears coming down her cheeks. She just couldn't believe what she was hearing from her lawyer.

Sonya exclaimed, "What.....what.....oh my god....I just can't believe it".

Mr. Brown got up from his chair to shake her hands, and said, "Congratulations to you and Shahil."

Trembling, Sonya took his hands, and whispered, "How can I ever thank you? You did a great job. We have been struggling to prove his innocence for so many years. Thank you, thank you so...much....."

Mr. Brown: Remember, Ms. Mehra, a eye witness could make mistake in identifying some one as he or she is human being. But solid evidence like tire trace couldn't be wrong.

Sonya sat back on her chair and leaned back to feel peace. She closed her eyes for a moment, as she still couldn't believe what she had heard.

Mr. Brown explained that Shahil would be released in a month or so, as they had to take care of some paperwork. Sonya was very happy at the moment and in peace; she realized it was not a dream anymore.

She got up to leave her lawyer's office. Sonya hugged the lawyer as he was another angel in her life.

Sonya came home that evening screaming in joy, "Finally, we have won." She called Suri and Krish, and hugged them. Suri and Krish didn't understand why their mom looked so happy. Sonya said, "Dad will be back home within a month or so." Suri and Krish jumped out of joy as they were also waiting to see dad for long time.

Sonya called her family friends and even her own family members back home. While, she was eagerly waiting to hear from her lawyer about the release date, she started to dream as what she would do after Shahil comes home. She started to plan for long vacation trips.

44. Shahil at home

It was almost 10:30 p.m. at night. Sonya was playing a game with the kids, when she heard a knock on the door. Sonya ignored it first, but when she heard it again, she wondered who it might be that late at night.

She was scared, but she went to the door.

"Who is it?" Sonya asked.

"It's me, Sonya." She couldn't recognize the voice, but it seemed familiar.

She asked again, "Who is it?" ...."Who is it?"....... "It's me, Sonya. It's me..... Shahil..... Shahil......."

Sonya was so surprised to hear his name and quickly opened the door. It really was Shahil standing at the front porch.

Shahl........Shahil......Shahil.......Sonya was screaming in surprise to see him all of a sudden. She hugged him for a long time. She starred at him for a while thinking it's not a dream. How Shahil would be there without any phone call! Sonya thought she was waiting for her lawyer to call her for the release date and Shahil was already released. She asked Shahil as why he didn't tell her, so she could have come to receive him.

Shahil told her that he wanted to surprise her and he told the lawyer not to give her a release date. Sonya was surprised and said, "oh, my god, you are something". Sonya kissed him couple times in the joy to see him surprisingly.

She brought him inside the house. As Shahil saw the kids, he hugged them dearly.

As Sonya's mom came downstairs, she was surprised to see Shahil. Shahil greeted her and knelt to touch her feet as a sign of respect.

Sonya's mom said with tears in her eyes, "Look at him, he hasn't changed at all. He still has his original way to respect the elderly". Everybody laughed.

Krish was hiding behind the door; he was afraid as he wasn't familiar with his dad. Shahil pulled him out, took him on his lap and kissed him a couple times. Krish hid his face on his chest, feeling comfort of having his Dad around.

45. Mom's b'day

The next few days passed by filled with laughter and happiness. Sonya called some of her family friends for dinner. They would chat until late into the night. They played cards, watched movie, told jokes and laughed. Shahil entertained them with good and bad experiences. They decided to have a day trip with all the friends.

Sonya and Shahil kept getting phone calls from their family overseas to visit home as soon as possible. Sonya's family was eager to see her two kids and Shahil's family was curious to see Sonya, Shahil, Suri and Krish. No one had seen Krish yet other than in photographs. Sonya and Shahil decided to visit home in the summer.

Shahil felt very grateful to Sonya's mom as she took care of his two kids and Sonya in the time of fear, anxiety and danger. Shahil wanted to do something for her, but was unable to decide. Sonya knew that her mom was turning 65 in a few months. So, she suggested celebrating her 65th birthday. Shahil liked her idea, and suggested that it should be a surprise birthday party only. Sonya expressed her problem as how they would be able to surprise her if she would be in the house. Shahil told her the idea. He would take her to New York to her cousin's house and would leave her there for week or so. That way they could prepare the party without her knowledge. Meanwhile they also booked their tickets to visit their family in India.

Every evening after work and on the weekends Sonya and Shahil went to the mall and stores for shopping. They purchased beautiful gift items such as clothes, jewelry, perfumes as well as other items. They packed their suitcases as they were buying. Sonya bought many clothes for herself and the kids. Occasionally, she remembered the night before they were about to leave a few years ago, and she became uneasy.

The summer season was approaching fast. The kids were ready for their summer vacation. A month before their trip, they started to shop for grandma's birthday celebration. Sonya sent birthday invitations to all her friends and to her mom's all friends too. She ordered food from the catering service and she bought lots of snacks and party supplies. About a week before the party, Shahil took her to her cousin's house for one week. Sonya's mom didn't want to go anywhere without the kids. She would miss them a lot, but Shahil said that she needed a break.

Shahil put the ribbons all around the house and put up the banner saying "65th Birthday". Lots of balloons were hanging from the ceiling. Shahil was at his best in decorating the house when it's a party time. Shahil made sure everything was in place. They picked up the cake order. He wanted to make Sonya's mom so happy that she would forget the pain from the last couple years. Shahil called the cousin in New York to bring her back home.

It was a beautiful and bright morning. Sonya kept the tables ready with snacks and plates. She made sure the catering service would arrive on time. Krish and Suri filled up few balloons with confetti, ready to blow up at the door. Almost all invited guest had arrived by 4:30 p.m. While they were having soda and snacks, they eagerly waiting for the birthday person to arrive.

Half an hour later, Sonya's cousin's car stopped in her driveway. All the guests had parked their car away from Sonya's house, so her mom wouldn't notice anything. Sonya's mom started to walk towards the main entrance. As she was coming, everyone was watching from the window and Shahil turned off the lights.

As she rang the door bell, Shahil opened the door. Once she entered the house, the lights were turned on, and everybody shouted "surprise." Krish and Suri threw their balloons filled with confetti.

For a moment, she was confused. She saw many guests wishing her "Happy Birthday." Then she started to cry out of joy. Many of her aged guests hugged her. After much chatting and laughter, she was ready to cut the cake. Suri and Krish were both at her side. She lighted the candle. Everybody sang "Happy Birthday," and she blew out the candles. The cake and snacks were served to each guest. After dinner, she opened all gifts. Everybody could see happiness gleaming in her eyes. Sonya and Shahil hugged her and thanked her for everything.

It was a happy memory for her mom, as she had been in the situation along with Sonya. Sonya's mom thanked Sonya and Shahil for thinking of her.

Now the whole family was eagerly waiting for their trip. All the preparations were done and the bags were packed. A week later, they left to visit their family in India.

46. Family back home

The stewardess announces, "Fasten your belts please. Fasten your belts. The plane is landing at the Bombay airport in a few minutes."

Sonya hears the announcement and blinks to make sure she is really on the plane. Will she finally be lucky enough to see her family members after ten years? She closes her teary eyes briefly, and then gets up to go to the restroom.

Shahil wakes up after hearing the announcement. The children are still sleeping with a pillow around their neck. He wakes up the children and tells them to get ready. They can't wait to get out and meet their relatives.

Air India 101 lands at the Sahara Airport in Bombay. The luggage is checked out and they proceed to go to the waiting area where all the family members are ready to receive them.

As they walk towards the waiting area, they see a big crowd of family members from both Sonya and Shahil's family. Everyone is eager to receive them with a bouquet of flowers. From far away, they can recognize mischievous little Krish and Suri as they were teasing each other and running after each other without noticing any family member. Everybody waves and shouts Shahil's name.

Sonya and Shahil hug their brothers and sisters, and many other family members. Tears of joy run down their faces. Krish and Suri met them for the first time, so everyone tries to catch their attention and showers them with hugs and kisses.

The family limousine started to run towards their home. In the limousine,. Sonya and Shahil holding their hand, are watching the pink sun just starting to rise early in the morning. They are looking forward to live happily ever after.

About the Author

Presently, settled in Pennsylvania. Lives with husband and two children.

Printed in the United States
By Bookmasters